WAR SMOKE

In Nevada, in the town of War Smoke, Marshal Matt Fallen is faced with a series of horrific murders. Someone brutally clubs innocent men, women and children to death with their six-shooters. War Smoke is full of strangers — impossible to find the culprit. But when it reaches the point that each night another body is discovered, Fallen is determined to find the murderer . . . At sunset Fallen vows to get his man. A showdown is brewing. Fallen is ready.

*Books by Michael D. George
in the Linford Western Library:*

MICHAEL D. GEORGE

WAR SMOKE

Complete and Unabridged

LINFORD
Leicester

First published in Great Britain in 2009 by
Robert Hale Limited
London

First Linford Edition
published 2010
by arrangement with
Robert Hale Limited
London

British Library CIP Data

George, Michael D.
    War smoke.- -(Linford western library)
    1. Western stories.
    2. Large type books.
    I. Title II. Series
    823.9′2–dc22

2/16

    ISBN 978–1–44480–052–4

Published by
F. A. Thorpe (Publishing)
Anstey, Leicestershire

Set by Words & Graphics Ltd.
Anstey, Leicestershire
Printed and bound in Great Britain by
T. J. International Ltd., Padstow, Cornwall

This book is printed on acid-free paper

Dedicated with love to my eldest son James Michael George for helping his old pa. Thanks, Jim.

Prologue

There were many back in the East who thought that all the lawmen in the West were noble beings who never made a mistake. They also believed that the outlaws with infamous names who robbed and killed in towns were simply Robin Hood characters. The dime novels had a lot to do with it. They romanticized everything far beyond their own boundaries.

In truth there was no black and white beyond the Pecos, where the Wild West was reputed to begin. It was a land filled with countless shades of grey. Men from both sides of the law were all different and none of them actually knew why he had become what he was.

The war had a lot to do with it, some said. A bitter twist of fate had made beggars of rich men and created a race of people who had seen so much pointless death that they could no longer see a future for themselves.

It was live for the day for there might never be a tomorrow.

Entire lives had changed as blue fought grey for a cause of which few knew the origins.

But when men are taught how to kill with no emotion they can change without ever knowing it. Thousands had survived the horrors of the brutal hostilities which had gone on for what seemed like an eternity. Some had managed to rebuild their lives in the new climate but others had not.

When you can kill without even feeling the slightest hint of guilt, and you have returned to nothing but the embers of the life that had existed before, some men choose to continue killing.

Being a lawman in the West was not a job most sane creatures would have chosen for themselves but some men did it for reasons that most kept to themselves.

Marshal Matt Fallen was such a man. He answered no questions concerning his life before he pinned on a tin star. And he had worn it now for more than a decade.

Fallen had managed to avoid the war, for its poison had not reached the desolate ranges of Nevada where he had spent every single day of his thirty-eight years. But as the years rolled on after the conflict ended the lawman felt the cancer of the bitter war start to invade and engulf his life and the town he proudly protected.

Evil rode many different horses.

It could dwell behind the scars of a face that had lived a tough existence as well as hide behind the angelic features of a choirboy.

Over the previous couple of years its presence had grown like a contagion.

Each day seemed to bring a new gunman into the remote settlement. Another man who wanted to prove himself and hire out to anyone willing to pay.

But there was something else besides the invasion of unwelcome riders that troubled the tall lawman. Once he had known everyone in town. Now his streets were filled with faces he did not recognize. Faces of hardened gunfighters swamped his once peaceful town. Their number grew steadily.

Now Fallen found that in his every waking moment he was called upon to uphold the law. So many guns in the hands of so many people whom he simply did not know. So many fights and potential showdowns cropped up in almost every street where there was either a saloon or a gambling house.

Tempers were frayed.

Then something else happened. It was not a mere killing. Not a shoot-out between men with smoking six-guns in their hands. It was more like a slaying. It was as if someone had decided to rid the town of innocent people in the most hideous of ways. What confused Fallen the most was that no bullets had been used.

For a gun can kill in many ways.

What faced Matt Fallen now was something that totally confounded him. All his years as an upholder of the law gave him no answers to the thousands of silent questions his mind posed.

There was someone in town who used his six-shooter to kill in a way that the lawman had never witnessed before. Men, women and even children had fallen victim to the maniac. Each had been bludgeoned until they were unrecognizable.

Each morning brought a new victim.

Fallen knew that he had to find the murderer fast before he struck again.

But how?

1

War Smoke was a dust-trap of a town situated on the dry banks of a river that had quit flowing a few years earlier. Yet the water in its wells remained sweet and the population still thrived against odds which no riverboat poker-player would have raised a bet upon. As its name implied, War Smoke was situated in a land once dominated by nomadic Sioux, who had long since disappeared to the high forested mountains far to the west. Yet even without the threat of the once regular Indian attacks, the town had not grown any safer.

For now there was a different threat.

There had been a while when peace had reigned in War Smoke and its immediate vicinity. It had lasted a few years and then suddenly a new sort of forewarning manifested itself. This was to prove a far more dangerous threat than any the Sioux had ever posed.

In all the town's history the law had managed to hold a tight grip on War Smoke in the hands of a strong, uncompromising marshal named Matt Fallen.

For nearly ten years Fallen had always dished out a simple but fair form of justice. It was said that half the plots on Boot Hill were filled with the men who had gone up against the old-fashioned lawman. Yet he had never once drawn his weapons on anyone who had not deserved it. Unlike so many other men who wore tin stars, Matt Fallen was a true upholder of the law.

A decade had seen War Smoke become one of the safest towns west of the Pecos, but suddenly things had changed.

Fallen was troubled.

His once peaceful town had started to get ornery and return to the way it had been when he had first sworn his oath of office.

During the previous twelve days he had seen a dozen or more of War Smoke's citizens murdered in a way that turned even his seasoned guts.

Fallen knew that there was more than one way that a six-shooter could be used to maim or slay but he had never seen the results so brutally displayed before. Most men who carried a hogleg used its trigger to spew out lead, but the victims of this carnage had been clubbed to death by someone who chose to use the butt or barrel of his gun to destroy life.

A single instance might have suggested that the killer wanted to make as little noise as possible but continuing to do it made no sense to a sane mind.

And why kill so many seemingly innocent folks?

The question dogged the marshal.

Fallen rose from the cot in his office next to the three jail cells and rubbed his eyes as he listened to the deputy unlocking the door. It was a new day and a new month and the marshal had barely had any sleep at all after walking the streets of the busy town until just before dawn.

He had tried to keep a vigil and protect those who relied upon him until weariness had forced him to return to his office. He glanced at the wall clock. It was nearly seven. He had slept for only an hour.

'Elmer!' Fallen said sleepily.

'Howdy, Marshal!' the deputy said cheerfully. 'Nice day ahead by the looks of it!'

Fallen swung his long legs over the edge of the crude bed and sat upright. He sighed, leaned down and pulled on his boots. 'Get the coffee on, Elmer! I've gotta try to wake up!'

Elmer Hook was nearly thirty and one of the most loyal men who had ever worked for Fallen. His only fault was that he was always happy and that could take its toll on a tired man.

'You bin patrolling the streets all night again, Marshal?'

'Yep!' Fallen stood and yawned.

'Every single one of them!'

Elmer busied himself and got the blackened pot onto the stove in a well-rehearsed manner. 'You shouldn't ought to wear yaself out like this, Marshal. You looks awful these days.'

Fallen ran his hands through his black hair and then moved to the office window. He raised the blind and squinted out on to Front Street. As always the people were starting to go about their daily rituals.

'Thank you, Elmer.'

Elmer shrugged. 'I don't mean to sound nasty or the like but you sure have gotten some awful dark shadows under ya eyes. A man gotta have some sleep now and then, ya know. If'n ya keep going this way there won't be a bargirl in War Smoke that'll give ya the time of day. 'Cepting the ugly ones.'

'You're the one that chases the bargirls, Elmer,' Fallen said drily.

'Oh yeah!' Elmer blushed. 'But ya gotta take care of ya looks all the same.'

'I'd heard that myself.' Fallen opened

11

a drawer in his desk and pulled out a mirror. He hung it on a nail on the wall above his washbasin and looked at the tired reflection. 'I need a shave.'

'Ya sure do,' Elmer agreed and pushed some kindling into the belly of the stove until its flames rose. 'I do declare that I ain't never seen ya like this.'

Fallen filled the basin with cold water from a pitcher. 'I walked those streets all night, Elmer. If that cold-blooded killer was out there I reckon he knew that I was too. The sun started to rise and I came here. I was too tired to go to my room at the hotel.'

Elmer closed the door of the stove and looked at the man he respected more than any other he had ever met. He nodded.

'I bet that ya right. Ya scared him off. Even a killer as bad as this 'un is ain't dumb enough to try his hand when Marshal Fallen in on the prowl. Yep, I guess it's worth making yaself a mess for a good cause.'

'Worth losing a night's shut-eye over.' Fallen smiled, dipped his shaving brush into the cold water and then began to lather its bristles on a bar of soap.

'Right enough.' Elmer nodded again. 'Mind you, if'n I'd bin up all night I'd have gone to Casey's barbershop and had him put a hot towel over my face. Nothing personal, Marshal.'

His face covered in lather, Fallen opened his straight razor and then went to raise it to his cheeks. The sound of his name being shouted over and over again stopped him. He turned and faced his deputy.

'You hear that, Elmer?'

'I surely do.' Elmer walked to the window and leaned close to the panes of glass. 'A little kid is calling out ya name. He's headed this way, Marshal.'

Both men heard the sound of the boardwalk creaking as someone ran along its weathered surface.

The door-handle rattled and a youngster no more than ten years of age burst into the office. The boy's eyes were wide and his mouth open as he gasped for air.

'If it ain't little Timmy Cooper,' Elmer said with a smile. 'What ya in such a hurry for, Timmy?'

Timmy took two steps into the office and pointed. 'M . . . marshal Fallen?'

Fallen wiped the soap from his face, turned and stared hard at the child. 'What is it, Timmy? Spit it out!'

'B . . . body, Marshal!' Timmy blurted out. 'A dead 'un!'

Fallen swallowed hard, walked to the boy and leaned over slightly. 'Where, Timmy?'

'In the livery, Marshal. In one of the stalls.'

'Oh, deary me!' Elmer sighed. 'That's just awful!'

'Go home, Timmy!' Fallen said firmly. 'And tell your ma that I thank you kindly.'

The youngster turned on his heels and did as he was told.

Matt Fallen strode to his cot and strapped his gunbelt around his hips.

Then he walked to his hatstand pulled his Stetson down and placed it on his head.

'C'mon, Elmer!'

Both men walked out into the morning sunshine.

2

Morbid curiosity had returned for the thirteenth time in as many days and hung like the smell of death itself around the livery stable. Only a public hanging could have drawn more human flies to the scene of yet another murder within the boundaries of War Smoke. As always, women outnumbered the men and even children were not immune to the age-old frailty of wanting to see things best left unseen. With every passing second, as more people learned of the latest victim, the crowd grew.

Excitement, which could have come from a time when men wore the skins and furs of animals on their backs as they wrestled with no greater problem than how to make fire, went through War Smoke like a forest fire when it finds dry brush to consume. It showed how little human nature had altered in all the thousands of years that men had walked upright.

Only two men amongst so many others did not want to see the body, but they had not only to see it, they had to search its clothing for clues.

It was their job. That was what they were paid to do.

Front Street was long and wide with more than a score of side streets and alleys leading off it into tangled mazes. More streets ran along to the rear of the yards behind the main thoroughfare itself. War Smoke was big by any standards but a fit man could walk its every boardwalk in the space of two hours.

The livery stable was situated at the southern end of the town, behind a massive oak with branches that looked capable of holding the weight of the heftiest of steers. It had in its time supported the weight of many a hanged man without any problem.

Matt Fallen defied his own tiredness and strode towards it and the livery stable with his trusty deputy at his side. Neither man had spoken a word since leaving the office. Neither of them had anything left to say which he had not already said about the previous twelve victims.

As they walked with purpose in their every stride, other people ran to the livery as though it held some ancient magical surprise. The crowd had already become six deep outside the wooden building. Like vultures they hovered by its high, wide-open doors, bathed in sickening fervour.

'Look at them, Elmer!' Fallen growled angrily. 'Look at them! Men and women and even kids trying to get a look at the body. I reckon this is a damn sad day.'

'It's just curiosity, Marshal,' Elmer said. 'Folks are just naturally curious.'

'Curiosity killed the cat, Elmer,' Fallen spat as he parted the people and marched into the cool interior of the livery stable. Then he paused.

Clem Doyle, the liveryman, moved towards the two lawmen and rubbed his muscular neck with hands that looked capable of bending horseshoes. Sweat and grease made his arms shine as sunlight cast across his powerful form.

'Bad business, Marshal!' Doyle said. 'Upset the horses a whole heap, ya know.'

'Yep,' Fallen agreed. 'Horses are sensitive critters, unlike the folks out there, Clem.'

Elmer leaned close to the marshal and squinted up into his face. 'What cat would that be exactly, Marshal?'

Fallen did not reply to the deputy's question. He turned his attention to the burly figure.

'When did you find it, Clem?'

'When I opened up. About twenty minutes back,' Doyle answered. 'I had me a real drink last night and stayed over at the Mustang. Usually I gets my shut-eye up in the loft in the hay.'

Fallen knew the Mustang saloon well. It had the best liquor in War Smoke and the prettiest girls. 'Was the livery locked up last night?'

Doyle waved people back and pointed at the nearest door. Its padlock hung on a broken hinge from splintered wood.

'Someone broke in, Marshal. Someone who must have known I weren't here.'

'That's kinda interesting.' Elmer nodded and tapped his teeth with a thumbnail. 'Ain't it, Marshal?'

'Mighty interesting, Elmer,' Fallen agreed.

'Ya gonna move that carcass out of here soon, Marshal?' Doyle asked. 'The smell is starting to upset the horses.'

Fallen turned and narrowed his sore eyes. The sight which met them stopped him in his tracks as had that of each of the previous dozen victims.

'Lucky there weren't no horse in that stall, Clem,' Fallen said.

'There was last night, Marshal. A grey mare. Ain't seen it this morning though,' Doyle told him. 'By the looks of that body it helped the killer stomp that poor critter into the next world. Hoofmarks all over that body.'

'Oh deary me,' Elmer gulped when his eyes also fixed upon the thirteenth victim. 'This 'un is worse than the others, Marshal!'

Matt Fallen took a deep breath and mustered all his resolve. He walked away from the liveryman, across the dirt floor, then paused above the body. He gritted his teeth and knelt.

'Any idea who this is, Elmer?'

Elmer was two steps behind the marshal. 'I don't recognize the clothes, Marshal. Ain't much else left to hang a hat on, is there?'

'You're right.' Fallen pulled back the blood-soaked coat and searched the pockets. 'Maybe we can find something that might have a name on it. If not we might find a room key that'll lead us to a hotel and a name on a register.'

Elmer carefully knelt down on the opposite side of the lifeless body and poked his long thin fingers into the pants pocket closest to him.

'Here's something, Marshal.'

Fallen looked at the scrap of paper in

his deputy's shaking fingers. He reached out and took it.

'What is it?' Elmer asked.

'I ain't too sure,' Fallen replied. 'We'll check it out back at the office later.'

'Look, Marshal! There's a bulge in his coat your side,' Elmer indicated.

'What have we here?' The marshal managed to peel the bloodied coat open and scoop out a well-filled wallet. It was, like the corpse, a mess of gore. 'Reckon we'll have to wash this down before we can open it. Maybe then we'll find out who this poor critter was.'

Elmer tutted and waved a hand over the crumpled body. 'That old grey mare sure done some powerful damage to whoever this was, Marshal.'

Matt Fallen glanced at his deputy. 'The horse didn't stove his head in, Elmer. Another sort of animal did that. A two-legged one. Maybe he's one of those curious varmints that's hanging around outside here.'

Elmer Hook swallowed hard at the suggestion. 'Reckon it could be one of them, now ya mentions it.'

'You in here, Matt?' a familiar voice bellowed out across the expanse of the livery.

Both lawmen looked to the bumbling figure making his way through the crowd by the open stable doors. He carried a weathered medical bag in his left hand and a smoking pipe in the other.

'Over here, Doc!' Fallen called out.

Doc Theo Weaver ambled to the bloody scene, stopped and sighed. He poked the stem of the pipe between his teeth and shrugged at the sight.

'What was the point of sending for me? You don't need me, Matt. You need the undertaker. Ain't nothing here for me to do.'

Fallen stood and nodded at the man who barely reached five feet in height.

'Yep! I know! Just like all the others.'

The three men started to walk back towards the morning sunlight. As Fallen neared the crowd he pointed at four of the nearest men who were making up part of the crowd.

'You four can go in there and get a real good look at that body,' the Marshal snapped. 'Then you can pick it up and take it to the funeral parlour!'

The men did not argue.

They obeyed.

Weaver sucked on his pipe thoughtfully and was about to speak when the sound of gunfire echoed off the wooden buildings which surrounded the trio.

'Gunshots, Marshal!' Elmer gasped.

'I figured that.' Fallen drew his gun and started to run. 'C'mon, Elmer!'

3

Lethal lead deafened and cleared Front Street within seconds of trouble erupting. It continued until the smoking chambers of the cowboys' guns were empty and they were forced to reload. The acrid scent of gunsmoke drifted across the sandy thoroughfare as War Smoke's citizens ran for cover. A sickening haze hung across Front Street, like phantoms seeking out a final resting place. The shots had come thick and fast but so far none of the deadly lead had found its target. Three drunken cowboys on the porch of the Golden Garter saloon held their smoking weapons in gloved hands as their fingers tried to shake spent casings loose and push fresh bullets into their six-shooters. Each stared out across the wide expanse of sand to the War Smoke gaming house, now hidden by the smoke.

'Did we hit 'em?' one asked.

'Must have!' another quipped.

'Reckon?' the third queried.

But none of the eighteen bullets which had spewed from the barrels of the cowboys' three six-guns had managed to find their chosen targets.

Two men dressed in clothing which would have not been out of place on the finest of Mississippi riverboats had taken refuge behind sturdy, well-filled water troughs. They knew who had opened up on them. And they also knew why.

'You boys had better quit your shooting, ya hear?' one of the gamblers called out.

'No need for killing, boys!' the other added.

The smoke lifted as a breeze traced down the centre of the street. For a moment all five men stared at one another. Then the shooting started again.

Dandy Jim Larsen and Ace Marsden had found themselves the chosen targets as they had left the gaming house after four straight hours of playing five-card stud poker. It did not come as too much of a shock to the pair of Southern gentlemen. In their chosen profession it was something they had gotten used to.

Men with fingers and hands capable of such manipulation of a deck of cards often used their skill to cheat. Sometimes their victims noticed, other times it took a while for the truth to dawn upon their victims.

Marsden and Larsen knew that on this occasion it was the latter.

Cowhands from the Lazy D cattle ranch were not the best at holding their tempers. Johnny Brewer and his brothers Ike and Dabs might not have been the brightest of men but they were honest and thought all others were the same. It shamed and hurt their kind when they realized that they were wrong. Totally wrong. They had brooded and waited for hours to unleash their venom on the pair of gamblers they knew had cheated them.

Each of the cowboys had seen a month's hard-earned wages disappear into the pockets of the gamblers.

Fuelled by more whiskey than was good for them the three young men had drifted away from their original plan of beating up Larsen and Marsden towards using them for target practice.

But unlike the many gunfighters in War Smoke who knew how to kill with perfection, the cowboys seldom used their weaponry.

The façade of the gaming house was riddled with bullets which had killed only termites.

Yet Johnny, Ike and Dabs kept fanning their gun hammers and shouting out at the men who had taken refuge behind the water trough.

'You cheatin' bastards are gonna die!' Ike yelled as he tried to take aim but ended up shooting into the sand instead. His brothers' lead carried across the street but still came nowhere close to finding the men who had pocketed not only their money but that of half a dozen other victims as well.

Larsen glanced to his left at Marsden.

'I told you them cowpokes would be trouble, Ace!'

Marsden drew the slim .38 from the holster hidden under his left armpit and cocked its hammer.

'Sure enough! But I told ya that we should have gone out the rear door, Dandy Jim!'

Bullets tore at the rim of the trough. Splinters showered over the pair of crouching men.

'Their lead is getting closer!' Larsen spat through the fine sawdust which had covered him.

'I say we finish them and ride out of this one-horse town and head to Virginia City,' Marsden suggested. 'They got some real money in Virginia City.'

Both men nodded. Their guns were ready.

They rose and began shooting.

4

Unable to contain their anger the three cowboys blasted their guns across the wide expanse of Front Street. Cowboy Johnny Brewer staggered to the nearest wooden upright and trained his gun on Larsen. Even the whiskey and the gunsmoke could not mask the face of the gambler who had, against the odds, somehow managed to find four kings to beat his quartet of queens.

Johnny squeezed his trigger just as Dandy Jim fanned the hammer of his own .45. The cowboy felt the heat in the centre of his chest and was thrown back against the saloon wall. No mule could have kicked harder. For a moment he did not realize what had happened and went to drag his gun hammer back again, but there was no strength remaining in his fingers or thumb.

Then Johnny saw Ike buckle as one of the gamblers' bullets caught his brother dead centre. Ike's gun blasted a hole into the boardwalk as he fell to his knees. Horses tied to a hitching rail tore at their reins and fled.

Horrified, Dabs started to scream and went to the aid of his siblings when he too was hit in his chest. The youngest of the Brewer brothers crashed into the Golden Garter's wall.

Stunned, Johnny began to cough as he raised his arm to fire his pistol. His eyes narrowed and focused on the blood splattering from his mouth over his shirtsleeve. He looked down and saw the hole in his shirt and the unexpected mess of red.

'I've bin hit!' he gasped. Neither of his brothers was capable of answering, for they had also taken lead.

Dabs was on his knees. He kept firing his gun at the ground until there were no more bullets left in the smoking-hot chambers. Johnny began to walk towards his brothers when he saw Ike's head jerk back violently. The gun fell from his brother's fingers, then he rolled across the boardwalk.

Johnny Brewer blinked hard. A pain like none he had ever experienced ripped through him as his mind suddenly began to accept the fact that he, like Ike and Dabs, had been skewered by a deadly accurate bullet.

Dabs was mumbling as he rocked on his knees.

'Dabs?' Johnny called out piteously.

Then Dabs's head exploded as one of Marsden's lethal bullets caught him above the left eye. Johnny slipped on the scarlet gore which was everywhere and fell beside his brothers. The cowboy looked up and saw the pair of fancy-dressed gamblers laughing at him. Johnny crawled over Ike's back and then saw Dandy Jim Larsen raise his arm and train the barrel of his gun on him.

A circle of smoke was the last thing the cowboy would ever see. His neck snapped as the impact of the well-placed bullet caught him between his eyes. He slumped over his blood-drenched siblings.

All three Brewer brothers lay lifeless on the porch of the Golden Garter saloon. Steam rose from the warm blood.

For three of the Lazy D cowhands, it was over.

Even the long legs of Matt Fallen were not capable of reaching Front Street in time to prevent the carnage which he and Elmer discovered to their horror as they raced towards the Golden Garter from a side street. Both lawmen slowed, then stopped when their eyes lit upon the streams of blood running down from the saloon board-walk.

'Oh deary me, Marshal!' Elmer said.

Fallen inhaled loudly. He focused on the red gore which was splattered across the wall and window of the saloon. The deputy kept walking until he was leaning over the dead men sprawled on the weathered boards.

'It's the Brewer boys, Marshal!'

Elmer gasped and looked to Fallen. 'They're all dead!'

'I know that, Elmer,' Fallen sighed.

Elmer rushed back to the side of the tall marshal and tapped his arm. Then he pointed at Larsen and Marsden.

'Reckon they're the galoots that done this! I never done trusted anyone who dresses up when it ain't Sunday, Marshal. Yep, I reckon they're the ones we want.'

Fallen dragged his gaze from the Brewer brothers and glared at the pair of gamblers opposite. Smoke still trailed from their gun barrels.

'The guns in their hands kinda give the game away as well, Elmer,' Fallen said.

'To tell the honest truth I never noticed the guns, Marshal.'

'Why did you kill these boys?' Fallen shouted at the gamblers as his deputy wandered back to the bodies. 'They were just dumb cowboys.'

Dandy Jim Larsen shrugged.

'Self-defence, Marshal.'

'They started it.' Marsden added.

Matt Fallen gritted his teeth and marched across the sand towards the men standing behind the water trough. He stopped, raised his left boot and rested it on the rim of the trough. He pushed the brim of his Stetson back off his brow and stared with venomous eyes at both gamblers.

'Like I said, they were just cowboys,' Fallen said drily. 'Neither of them could hit the side of a barn with a scattergun.'

'Cowboys or not, they started it,' Larsen repeated his friend's words. 'They were waiting for us out here and began shooting at us. When their bullets started to close in on us we had to stop them.'

'We just wanted to stop them,' Marsden nodded. 'Ain't our fault we happened to kill them.'

'You could have winged them,' Fallen said bluntly. 'There was no need for any killing. I don't like folks that kill when they could just as easily wing a varmint.'

'It was either them or us,' Larsen smiled.

Elmer had inspected the bodies more thoroughly and had moved across the street to the marshal's side again. He stared at the gamblers.

'You must be mighty fine shots by the way ya grouped them bullets together, gents.'

Fallen glanced at his deputy.

'Heart shots?' he queried.

Elmer nodded. 'And head shots as well. I never seen such accurate grouping, Marshal. Kinda frightening.'

Matt Fallen returned his eyes to the pair of well-dressed gamblers. He held out his left hand to Larsen and Marsden and glared at them.

'Give us those guns!' he ordered.

'Why, Marshal?' Marsden protested.

Faster than either of the men could believe, they saw Fallen's right hand draw, cock his gun and aim it straight at them.

'Why? Because I said so! Don't force me to kill you sidewinders before I've had me some breakfast! Now hand them guns over!'

Elmer leaned forward. 'I'd give Marshal Fallen ya guns real quick like, because he surely will kill ya otherwise. He ain't had much sleep and he's a tad ornery.'

Reluctantly Dandy Jim Larsen and Ace Marsden gave the guns to Fallen and Elmer. Only then did Fallen return his own weapon to its holster.

'That was the smartest thing you've done today,' Fallen muttered as he checked out the gun grip.

'What ya looking at the grips for?' Larsen asked.

'Somebody bin crushing skulls in War Smoke,' Fallen answered slowly. 'It wasn't you, though.'

'This 'un is as clean as a whistle as well, Marshal,' Elmer nodded.

Larsen sighed. 'Me and my partner want to ride out of this town and head off to Virginia City, Marshal. Any objections?'

Fallen considered the question. 'Maybe.'

Elmer opened the gun and uttered in

surprise, 'Only three shots bin used, Marshal!'

Fallen did the same to Larsen's gun. 'Same here.'

'What's wrong?' Larsen asked sheepishly.

'Three dead men with a bullet in each heart and each head takes a lot of skill, men,' Fallen said. 'Most times when folks are being shot at they return fire blindly. You two placed your bullets exactly where you wanted them and each of you had three rounds spare. I find that kinda troubling.'

'It was self-defence,' Marsden growled. 'You can't hold us for anything. Those cowpunchers started it. Me and Dandy Jim just finished it. That's it.'

Fallen could see the townspeople starting to reappear all around them. He bit his lip, grabbed the gun from his deputy's hands, then threw both weapons into the trough that stood between himself and the gamblers. Then he squared up to the fancy pair.

'What a shame! Nothing worse than wet guns!'

Larsen and Marsden watched silently as bubbles rose from their pistols to the surface of the water. Both men recognized the fury blazing in the eyes of the marshal as he turned away from them and gave a glance at the three dead bodies again.

'C'mon, Elmer! Let's go get us some coffee. I got me a real bad taste in my mouth I wanna try and wash away.'

'Can we leave War Smoke?' Dandy Jim Larsen managed to ask.

Fallen looked over his shoulder as he and Elmer headed back down the street in the direction of his office.

'Sure! But you had better ride damn fast!' Fallen said in a cold voice capable of freezing the blood in most men's veins.

Marsden removed his coat and rolled up a sleeve. 'Why? You figuring on following us, Marshal? You the kind that makes ya own kind of law outside the boundaries of town?'

'Not me, mister,' Fallen replied with a low drawl. 'I ain't gonna waste time trailing vermin. But I'm sure the rest of the Lazy D cowboys will follow you when they find out about this. Johnny and his brothers were pretty well liked. You made three big mistakes and I figure you'll pay the price. *Adios!*'

'You'd send them after us?' Larsen called out.

'Damn, right!' Fallen yelled back.

Marsden dipped his hand into the cold water and brought up one gun at a time. He and his fellow gambler looked at each other and then back at the two lawmen, who continued walking down the long wide street.

'What we gonna do, Dandy Jim?' Marsden asked as he shook his sodden .38. 'What the hell are we gonna do?'

Dandy Jim Larsen sighed. 'Ride as fast as we can, Ace!'

5

The aroma of gunsmoke still hung in the air along the entire length of Front Street. Yet the horseman who had just entered War Smoke either did not notice or did not care. His nostrils were used to the smell of death. It had become part of him.

Hudson Parker had been many things in his twenty-nine years. But the thing he was best at was killing. Parker, like so many others who had found themselves caught up in the Civil War had discovered that he was not only a good shot with both gun and rifle, he also had no conscience. He could kill anything or anyone without the slightest twinge of guilt or remorse. His name and reputation were well known across Texas, but to those in Nevada he was just another gunfighter. Another one of those forced further afield to ply his trade and earn his blood money.

His tall, lean frame was hidden by a long trail-coat which bore evidence of the many lethal encounters Hudson Parker had engaged in and won. Like so many of his contemporaries Parker had been drawn north by the rumour that there were many cattle ranchers who would willingly pay far more than he could expect for his deadly services back in his native Texas.

Homesteaders were now fencing off the vast grass ranges and this had already brought them into brutal conflict with the rich ranchers.

Some had decided to take the law into their own hands.

Men like Parker were more than willing to use their ruthless abilities if the money was right. They did not question why certain people had to be gunned down. They just accepted the golden eagles and did it.

Parker, unlike so many of the other well-heeled gunmen who had started to gather in War Smoke, rode alone. He did not mix well at the best of times and since the war he had refused to allow anyone to get close to him. Knowing people was bad enough. Actually liking people was far worse.

The lathered-up mount was turned towards the nearest of the many saloons in War Smoke and given a final jab of the sharp spurs. It trotted up to the Golden Garter's façade and snorted as it sensed the lingering smell of death.

Hudson Parker drew rein and dismounted outside the Golden Garter. He stared coldly at the blood and body fragments which still covered the boardwalk and stained the sand. The saloon was now getting busy as the morning sun slowly reached its zenith in the cloudy blue sky.

Hec Jones, the barkeep, came through the swing doors of the saloon and tossed a bucket of soapy water over the red gore. He glanced at the painfully thin gunfighter as Parker looped his reins over the hitching rail pole.

'Ya missed one hell of a shoot-out, stranger!'

Parker barely acknowledged the remark as he knotted the reins and stepped up on to the wet boards. The gunfighter looked every inch the killer that he had become. He stood tall with the long trail-coat's tails flapping in the gentle breeze which traced along Front Street. His guns gleamed in their holsters and his hands never moved far from their grips. It was obvious to Jones that a different kind of hired gun had entered War Smoke. Parker pulled a long, thin cigar from his vest pocket and placed it between his teeth before striking a match with the thumbnail of his left hand. The gunman inhaled and looked over the swing doors.

'Open for business?'

'Yep!' Jones cleared his throat and cautiously allowed the man to enter before him. He followed at a distance he knew would not give the gunfighter any call to turn the magnificent weaponry on him.

The sound of the bloodstained spurs echoed off the dry wooden walls and alerted the other men inside the Golden Garter to his deadly presence.

'Drink?' Jones asked as he dropped the bucket and walked behind the long bar.

Parker stopped, glanced around at the faces of the dozen or more other men in the dark saloon and nodded.

'Whiskey?' Jones asked.

Again Parker nodded.

'Ain't very talkative, are ya?' Jones said as he plucked a bottle off the shelf behind him and pulled its cork.

The eyes of the gunfighter rose to stare straight at the balding Jones. If death had a face, Jones thought, it was this one.

'You got law in this town?' Parker asked.

'Sure have,' Jones replied. 'One of the very best.'

Parker kept staring at the barman. 'What they call him?'

'Matt Fallen. Marshal Matt Fallen. Ya

ever heard of him, stranger?'

Hudson Parker nodded. He had heard the name and of the reputation of Fallen on his journey to this place. Fallen was unlike many lawmen whom he had encountered since the end of the war. Fallen was said to be a real law officer. Not the sort to be easily bribed or frightened.

'There ain't nobody ever gotten the better of Matt!' Jones enthused. 'Nope! He's so fast that he could have made a fortune if'n he'd ever strayed to the other side of the law. I bet he's even faster than they say Jesse James is. I bet he is, ya know?'

'You ever stop talking, little man?' Parker muttered in a low deathly drawl. 'You ought to stop talking. You might just live a little longer.'

Hec Jones felt his heart quicken. He went to apologize and then thought better of it. He placed a shining thimble glass down and filled it with the amber liquor.

Parker leaned across the counter,

snatched the whiskey bottle with one hand and flicked a couple of coins at the barkeep with the thumb of the other.

Jones swallowed hard. Again he did not speak.

The gunfighter tossed the whiskey into his mouth, then refilled the glass. He repeated the action and then pushed his coat-tails over the holstered guns.

A muted gasp rose up from the men sitting around the saloon as their eyes saw the deadly shooting-rig. Each of them knew that whoever the thin man was, he was a professional. They all knew that no mere amateur could have afforded that sort of lethal rig.

'You know a critter named Bruno Jackson?' Parker asked as his eyes surveyed the other patrons of the Golden Garter.

Jones nodded slowly and his eyes kept staring at the guns and the hand-tooled belt which faced him.

'He owns the Bar Q spread.'

Parker filled the glass again. 'He rich?'

Jones nodded firmly. 'Yep.'

The gunfighter smiled. 'Good.'

'Ya know Bruno?' Jones enquired.

'Nope, but I will,' Parker said. 'I surely will.'

★ ★ ★

The wall clock in the marshal's office chimed. It was noon and so far the tally of bodies in town was up to four. A seated Matt Fallen rested his head on his wrists and inhaled the steam from his coffee cup as Elmer continued to busy himself around the office. The deputy knew that all his words had been wasted as the marshal fought off his tiredness and tried to work out what he could do to stop the carnage that had struck War Smoke.

'Ya looks plumb tuckered, Marshal,' Elmer noted as he swept dust from around the marshal's boots. 'Why don't ya get a few hours' shut-eye on the cot?'

'Maybe you're right,' Fallen said.

Then the office door opened briskly and the sound of disgruntled men's voices filled the room. Fallen sat upright. His eyes focused on the three men who paraded in. They were the mayor and two of his flunkies.

Sol Hancock was a man closer to sixty than fifty. He was plump and wealthy from the profits on all the lumber he had sold and he had been mayor for nearly as long as Fallen had worn his tin star. He had a face which varied in shades of red depending upon how flustered he was.

The marshal could see that Hancock was almost crimson.

'Howdy, Sol.'

'What are you gonna do about this, Marshal?' Hancock shouted. He held a crumpled newspaper in his left hand which he waved as though it were a flag. 'This cannot go on! You must do something!'

'Stop waving that paper about, Sol,' Fallen said. 'What has gotten you all fired-up like this?'

'Read this!' Hancock slammed the paper down on the desk in front of the lawman and snorted. 'Read it!'

Fallen glanced up at the rotund figure and then looked at the paper. He began to flatten it with his hands. The ink was still fresh and stained his skin.

'It'd be a whole lot easier if you hadn't crushed the damn thing.'

Hancock pointed a finger at the headline. 'Read that! Read that and tell me how you think this is going to go down with folks!'

' 'Nevada town cursed by maniac killer!' ' Fallen read the headline aloud. 'Reckon that covers it OK.'

Elmer walked to the marshal's side and leaned on his broom as he read the story over the broad shoulder.

'My! That is a real spooky line and no mistake!'

Hancock dragged a chair across the floor and sat down opposite the marshal, across the desk.

'We can't let the outside world think

that there's a maniac killer in War Smoke, Matt,' Hancock wailed. 'It'll ruin our town for years to come.'

'There is, though,' Elmer piped up. 'Whoever's bin stoving them folks' heads in must be kinda unhinged.'

'Quiet, Elmer!' Fallen said. 'The mayor has a point. After all this ain't gonna be too good for business.'

Hancock mopped his face with a handerchief and nodded. 'My point exactly. The editor of the *Bulletin* has wired this story back East. This could ruin me!'

Fallen sighed. 'How? You're already the richest man in the state. I can see that folks might be a tad nervous coming here at the present time but — '

'You have to capture this maniac, Matt!' Hancock urged as he slammed his fist on the desk.

Fallen looked at the black coffee in his cup as it rippled, then he diverted his eyes to the almost purple face. 'I have bin trying to do just that, Sol. Ain't easy catching someone before they kills someone.'

'I've put up a thousand-dollar reward for the capture of this maniac, Matt,' Hancock said bluntly. 'If you can't catch the monster then maybe the folks in town will want to earn themselves a thousand dollars and do it for you.'

Fallen stood and waved his large hands at the mayor. 'No way, Sol! You can't do that!'

'It's my money!' Hancock snapped. 'I can do anything I like with it. I've already had the posters printed up.'

Fallen walked around the desk and rested a hip on the edge nearest to Hancock. He stared down at the sweating man.

'You don't understand. If you put up reward posters we'll have even more killings in War Smoke. Every idiot with a gun will be shooting the *hombre* nearest to him and try to make a claim for your money.'

Hancock rose to his feet. 'I'm sorry, Marshal. I have to act to restore confidence in our fair town before we're all ruined for good.'

'It's a loco idea,' Fallen said.

'I have boys putting the posters up as we speak,' Hancock told him. 'If you don't want people killing innocent strangers I suggest you do your job and find that evil killer first.'

Fallen watched as the three men marched out into the street. He lifted his cup and drank its entire contents in one long swallow.

'There's something fishy abut these killings, Elmer,' he said in a long sigh.

'What ya mean by fishy, Marshal?' Elmer took the cup, walked to the stove and refilled it.

Fallen stood and moved to the open doorway. His eyes narrowed and he studied the street carefully.

'I got me a feeling that this killer ain't a maniac after all, Elmer.' Fallen took the hot cup from his deputy and blew at the black beverage.

'He gotta be loco.'

'Or someone who wants everyone to think he is,' Fallen suggested.

'But why would anyone wanna make folks think he's as crazy as a loco bean, Marshal?' Elmer rested his weight on the broom and looked hard at his superior.

'There might be something more complicated behind this,' the marshal considered. 'We might be chasing someone who ain't crazy at all. Someone who is sane but real evil.'

'But who would kill so many folks just to fool us thataway, Marshal?'

Fallen glanced at Elmer. He smiled. 'When we figure that out I reckon we'll have this solved.'

Elmer shrugged. 'I think I'll put some lime in the outhouse.'

Fallen sipped at his coffee.

'That can wait. I've got a better idea, Elmer.'

6

Moose Coltrane was wide and strong and simple. Some said God had blessed him with the strength of three normal men in exchange for giving him the mind of a child. But to some that made him perfect. The fact was he had never been anything other than a human workhorse to those who had raised him. Found wandering alone out on the prairie two decades earlier by Bruno Jackson's cowboys, the child was fed only if he toiled.

Moose had worked hard for the begrudged scraps from the table of the Bar Q rancher. In fact he had never stopped working as his appetite grew along with his enormous frame.

No one knew exactly how old he had been when they discovered him. His size had said he was at least in his teens but his simple mind said he was far younger. Unlike his body, Moose's intelligence never grew and it appeared to be doomed to remain that of a infant.

Whatever had happened to the child's family was never ascertained. If Moose knew, he had never spoken of it. But the strong young man, who did the work of three men on the Bar Q ranch, never learned to speak more than the scattering of words he'd had at the time of his discovery.

Some thought that Bruno Jackson must be a kind and generous soul to have taken a stray waif into his home. Yet the truth was far less wholesome. The wealthy rancher had never allowed Moose inside his ranch or bunkhouses. Jackson treated his stock better than the young man.

Like an animal, Moose had found a place in the loft of the barn where he slept during the few hours of the day when he was not made to labour. But he never complained. It was not in his nature ever to think others were taking advantage of him. He always accepted his fate with a childlike smile.

Whoever the slow-witted strongman really was would probably never be determined. Jackson had not wanted to lose such a hard-working ranch hand and so he had not tried to find out the truth for fear of losing someone who worked for nothing.

Even the name of Moose Coltrane was unreal. Because of his size he had been called Moose by the other cowboys. The name of Coltrane had been on a scrap of paper in the child's pocket. It meant nothing and so was given to the child who also did not mean anything.

But even those with broken minds which were incapable of growing became men eventually. Moose was no different from all the other young men who lived in or around War Smoke.

He had needs but, unlike the majority of other young men, he did not understand what those needs were.

Moose had started to become more

and more unhappy and unsettled. Suddenly hard work no longer satisfied him as it had always done before. There had to be more. Even those who knew as little as Moose felt the season alter as spring returned.

Knowing that it was never wise to upset anyone as powerful as Moose was, Jackson realized that he had to try and keep his hardest working hand sweet.

The rancher had to head off the mood swings of the incredibly strong youngster before anything happened. Although he never lost his temper, Moose looked as though he could at any moment.

Moose might not have realized it but manhood had at last come to him.

Reluctantly, Jackson had given Moose a horse of his own. For a while this had calmed him down as he had galloped around the ranges south of the Bar Q. Then Moose became more daring. His veins were filled with the desire for adventure. Like a child exploring the limits of his own bravery, Moose rode further and further away from the heart of the Bar Q.

As the church-clock bell tolled to inform the residents that it was now one o'clock in the afternoon, the naïve Moose Coltrane rode into the back streets of War Smoke.

His eyes were wide in wonderment. This was a place he had never come to on his own. It was a place of magic to him. A place where so much always seemed to be happening. A place where bar-girls wore brightly coloured low-cut dresses.

To a youngster with the sap rising, this was heaven on earth.

For twenty years Moose had accompanied the other Bar Q cowboys into the busy town to collect supplies every month. They always brought him on the buckboard so that he could lift and carry the hefty sacks of provisions.

Now he was here on his own.

All the locals knew Moose by sight. They knew that he spoke little but was always polite and quiet. They also knew that he was incredibly strong and slow-witted.

As his mount walked slowly along the back streets the bareback horseman could not believe how many people were looking at him.

He smiled as always.

Moose Coltrane was confused when he realized that today few smiled back.

He would not have understood, even if anyone had explained it to him, that the town had fallen victim to a mysterious killer who battered skulls to pulp for no obvious reason.

The faces of those who watched the unusual sight of the large bareback rider entering their town only hours since the last body had been discovered in the livery stables now saw something they had never seen before.

They saw a strong young man with the mind of a child.

A man who could hardly communicate with others, Moose was no longer the object of their sympathy. Now he was something entirely different.

Something which made them uneasy.

Slow-wits could be and were considered insanity by most folks who had no idea that the majority of true maniacs looked completely normal.

The stories of the insane killer filled them with fear and trepidation. A whisper passed among those who witnessed the rider who joyfully rode through the back streets. A whisper that would soon become deafening.

There was a simplistic logic. Moose Coltrane could be called a maniac by those who did not know him. A thousand questions invaded the minds of those who had read the morning's newspaper and watched as the smiling figure rode slowly through War Smoke.

Could he have killed all those people?

They all knew of his feats of strength. Their eyes looked at the hands that held the reins. Big hands. Powerfully big hands which could crush anything. Even skulls.

The whisper grew louder. It spread like a contagion.

Moose kept smiling.

7

The old horse had seen better days. That was probably why Bruno Jackson had given it to Moose. But it could still gallop when urged and had a stamina most younger animals had yet to find. It was more horse than most and had pulled a buckboard for more than ten years before the rancher had invested in a matched pair of younger animals to replace it. But to Moose it was his prized possession. It was also his only possession. Few other horses could have carried the weight of Moose so effortlessly but to the nag it was far easier than pulling a fully laden wagon. Its sturdy legs rounded the corner and it made its way into Front Street. Its rider was still smiling as his eyes widened at all the colourful façades they focused upon.

Doc Weaver ambled along the board-walk and stopped outside the marshal's office. The door of the office was open and the deputy was seated on the steps down to the dusty street. Doc pulled a hardback chair away from the wall and sat down.

'Say, Elmer,' Doc started. 'When am I gonna get paid for all the work I've done?'

'What work would that be, Doc?' Elmer asked.

'What work? I've bin called out every time you boys have found a body with its head caved in. That work!' Doc snorted.

'But ya ain't done nothing 'cept say they was dead,' Elmer smiled,

Doc cleared his throat. 'That's a medical statement. Do you know that a man ain't legally dead unless a doctor says so?'

'Is that so?' Elmer shrugged.

'It is and it costs two dollars for each of them.' Doc nodded firmly.

'Well, glory be!' Elmer said, pointing

a finger at the sight of Moose riding down the centre of the long, wide street. 'Would ya look at that, Doc!'

'Hey, Matt!' Doc piped up over his shoulder. 'Come look at this!'

'Look at what, Doc?' Fallen asked. He stepped out into the afternoon sunshine and rested a hand on the nearest wooden upright.

Elmer pointed. 'There! That's young Moose.'

'That's Moose all right, on a horse,' Doc sighed.

Fallen nodded. 'Got himself a horse. Old Jackson must be mellowing in his old age.'

'Do ya reckon Jackson give it to him?' Elmer asked. He got to his feet and brushed down his britches with his hands.

'Could have given him a saddle as well,' Fallen observed.

Doc Weaver chuckled. 'Do they make saddles to fit boys that size, Matt?'

Elmer scratched his chest. 'Must be real odd to be like Moose, Marshal.'

'In what way?' Doc asked.

'To be kinda dumb, like.' Elmer looked at Doc and added. 'He always smiles, though. I've seen some of them Bar Q cowpokes whip him with the tails of their reins like he was a hound dog but he just smiles.'

'You smile a lot as well, Elmer,' Fallen pointed out.

Doc pulled out his pipe and blew down its stem. 'Pity there ain't more souls like Moose in this damn world, Elmer. Might be a nicer place if'n there was.'

'Sure enough.'

Fallen rested his thumbs on his gunbelt. 'Maybe he don't see the world like the rest of us, boys. Maybe he just don't see the hate and anger like we do.'

'Reckon not,' Elmer shrugged. 'He must see things that the rest of us are blind to. Look at him smile, Marshal. Warms ya heart, don't it?'

Fallen nodded. 'Reckon you might be right.'

Doc got back to his feet. 'When am I

gonna get my money for seeing them bodies, Matt? I figure War Smoke owes me twenty-six dollars so far.'

Fallen grinned and gestured to the open door. 'Come on into the office, Doc. I'll pay your blood money.'

Elmer started to laugh. 'Blood money! That's kinda funny, ain't it?'

The three men entered the office. No sooner had Moose ridden past the marshal's office than a deafening volley of shots rang out.

Matt Fallen drew his gun, cocked its hammer and ran back out on to the boardwalk. He crouched. His eyes darted in search of the gunman. Elmer skidded to a halt beside him.

Both men watched in stunned horror as the big horse with its big rider fell sideways down into the sand.

'Somebody done shot Moose, Marshal!'

Fallen gritted his teeth. 'Get your scattergun!'

Elmer dashed back inside as Doc cautiously edged out into the sunshine.

'I sure hope this is a job for me and ain't another one for the undertaker, Matt.'

Fallen did not reply.

The three men raced towards the stricken horse and its rider when another shot rang out from above the gaming house. The bullet hit Moose in his muscular left shoulder. Fallen swung round in mid-stride and blasted his Colt at the tell-tale plume of smoke he saw drifting from above the façade.

A Winchester went high as the lawman's bullet tore the deadly weapon from the hands of the gunman. Fallen squared up to the building and saw an unfamiliar man dressed in trail gear stagger away from the façade on the shingle roof.

The man had survived one bullet from Fallen but was not smart enough to leave it be. He drew a long-barrelled Remington .44 from a holster on his hip and went to aim.

Again Fallen squeezed his trigger.

This time there was no mercy in the marshal's lead.

The man took the bullet dead middle and folded up.

He fell head over heels off the roof and landed on top of a hitching rail. The weathered pole snapped as did the spine of the already dead man.

Dust rose up from the ground from the brutal impact.

It was the gunman's epitaph.

8

The crowd had gathered quickly around the bodies of the gunman and the innocent youth, which were separated by a mere twenty strides. They had come from all directions like flies to a fresh dung heap. Most had encircled the blood-soaked sand where the stricken horse and its master lay. The remainder buzzed around the unknown gunman who had probably only made two really bad mistakes in a lifetime of living by his gun. The first was to cut down Moose. The second and last was to attempt to shoot Matt Fallen.

Fallen pushed people aside forcefully and cleared a route to where Moose lay motionless in his own blood. Doc and Elmer went through the gaps in the crowd's shoulders to where they had a better view of Moose. Even unconscious the face still looked as though it were smiling.

Doc knelt beside Moose.

'He's still breathin', Matt.'

'Thank the Lord!' Elmer said as he held the hefty scattergun across his chest and eyed the people around them. 'Can ya save him, Doc?'

'I'll sure try.' Doc examined the massive frame.

Fallen walked to where the gunman lay. His eyes burned down at the man whom he had never seen before. He wondered why the stranger would have opened up on the hapless young man.

'Anyone know who this critter was?' Fallen yelled at the score of faces.

'And why did he shoot Moose?' Elmer added as he caught up to the marshal. 'It don't make no sense at all for anyone to shoot Moose.'

Fallen holstered his gun, leaned down and opened the man's coat to reveal a folded wanted poster. He stood back up and shook the poster open.

'What is it, Marshal?' Elmer asked.

'Just a wanted poster on some galoot

named Texas Tom McCree. I've never heard of him.'

'I never heard of him either, Marshal.' Elmer shrugged his shoulders with the scattergun clutched in his hands. 'Reckon this fella was a bounty hunter? Maybe this Texas Tom looks a bit like Moose to him?'

'The description don't fit, Elmer.'

'But do ya think he might be a bounty hunter?'

'Yep. He's a stinking bounty hunter all right. And I got me a feeling that he ain't the only one we got in War Smoke.' Fallen nodded as he strode back to where Doc was still kneeling beside the dead horse and its wounded master. 'Well, Doc?'

'He ain't dead yet, Matt,' Doc said as he struggled to get back to his feet. 'But he will be if'n I don't cut them bullets out of his hide as soon as I can. I gotta get him to my office fast.'

Fallen pointed at the nearest men in the crowd. 'Pick this boy up and take him to Doc's! And be smart about it!'

Like rookie soldiers faced with a burly parade-ground sergeant, the men obeyed without question and carefully lifted Moose up off the sand. They trailed the doctor back to his office. The marshal edged closer to Elmer.

'Go with them, Elmer,' Fallen said. 'I want Moose protected just in case some other half-witted fool tries his luck.'

'Right enough, Marshal,' Elmer nodded and ran after the men.

Matt Fallen turned and studied the faces of the remaining men and women, who were about to scatter. He raised his voice. They all froze in their tracks.

'I'll ask you all this just once. Why did that gunman do this to Moose?'

A rumble went around the men and women. Then Tom Dwyer, a sixty-year-old who tended bar in one of the back-street saloons ventured forward. He held a poster in his shaking hand.

'Maybe this is why, Marshal,' Dwyer said as he offered a brand-new poster to the tall man.

The marshal grabbed the paper and

stared at it. His face went red with rage. It was one of Sol Hancock's posters offering a $1,000 reward in bold black lettering. The reward was offered for capturing or killing the maniac killer. It was not too clear which deed would earn the money.

Fallen screwed the paper up and tossed it aside. He then saw more of the same in the hands of other members of the crowd.

'How many of these damn things are there?' Fallen yelled at them.

'Must be a thousand or more.' A woman pointed at the wooden uprights along the street. Fallen screwed up his eyes. His jaw dropped. It seemed as if each of them had a poster tacked to it.

The lawman exhaled loudly. 'Why would someone shoot Moose just because they seen one of these posters?'

'Moose ain't normal, Marshal.'

'He fits the description.'

'Who knows what someone like that could do?'

'His kind ought to be in an asylum someplace.'

Matt Fallen turned on his heels and looked at the people he thought he knew. Then another voice spoke. Fallen recognized it.

'That fool is too dangerous to be let into town.' The voice was that of Nate Bean. Bean owned at least a quarter of the gaming houses in War Smoke and had been buying up land meant for settlers west of town. He had a way of making the lawman angry just by being within whistling distance. Bean always smelled sweet. Too sweet for most folks' liking.

Fallen's eyes narrowed.

'You trying to justify Moose getting shot, Bean?'

'He is an idiot, Marshal,' Bean said smugly. 'Little better than an animal, Marshal. I can see how he could be mistaken for the monster who has bin killing folks in War Smoke.'

Fallen turned to the people gathered close. 'Listen up! Whoever killed all the local folks in town used the butt and barrel of a gun. That poor simple boy ain't never even owned or held a gun in his whole life.'

'You say a gun butt was used,' Bean commented. 'Can you prove that, Marshal?'

'I don't have to prove anything, Bean,' Fallen snarled. 'I seen all them smashed-up faces and skulls up close. On at least half of them you could see the clear outline of a gun grip and barrel markings on the flesh. Bruises.'

Bean stepped closer. 'I thought that dead people cannot get bruised skin?'

'You happen to be right and wrong, Bean.' Fallen clenched his fists at his side. He fought every instinct within him not to punch the man who stank of French perfume.

'How?'

'Because every one of the victims bruised up real bad before they were bludgeoned to death. It's true a dead person cannot bruise but them people were alive until the final few blows.

Now do you savvy?'

Nate Bean smiled and walked away from the lawman and the crowd. His aroma lingered.

'Moose couldn't have killed anyone,' Fallen said again. 'I reckon that this is the first time he's had the guts to ride into town from the Bar Q. By my figuring he ain't gonna do it again anytime soon. If he lives, that is.'

'But he's loco like the poster said,' a voice piped up from beyond the marshal's range of vision. 'Strong and loco.'

Fallen was now angrier than he had ever been before.

'Being slow and big don't make you a maniac or a killer.'

'Easy for you to say but ya can't prove Moose ain't the killer, Marshal,' another man heckled.

Fallen looked at the sun for a brief moment. Then he returned his eyes to the crowd.

'It'll be dark in five or six hours. If the maniac strikes again tonight that'll be proof enough.'

He turned. A hushed silence over-whelmed those in the crowd as his words sank into their collective mind. The scent of the perfume was replaced by that of fear. The people watched the tall, broad-shouldered lawman walk in the tracks left by the men who carried Moose to the doctor's office.

'Somebody go get the undertaker for the gunslinger and someone else can fetch Clem to drag that horse away,' Fallen shouted out.

The marshal had placed one boot on the boardwalk outside the doctor's office when he saw both of the gamblers he had thought were leaving town. They were walking from the High Top hotel towards one of Nate Bean's gaming halls, called The Dice.

Fallen diverted his stride and marched across the street. Their paths collided outside the hardware store.

Ace Marsden and Dandy Jim Larsen stopped and stared at the lawman.

'Anything we can do for you,

Marshal?' Larsen asked.

'I thought you two were headed west this morning,' Fallen said bluntly. 'What are you doing here?'

'We figured it was smarter to wait for the rest of those cowboys here than have them attack us on the trail,' Marsden answered.

Fallen sighed. 'You figuring on killing more cowpunchers?'

Both men smiled.

'If we do it'll be self-defence, Marshal,' Larsen said.

'Any trouble, Fallen?'

Fallen turned and saw Nate Bean standing outside The Dice.

'You're starting to get on my nerves, Bean.'

'Dandy Jim and Ace work for me,' Bean told him.

'Since when?'

'This morning.' Nate Bean opened the door to his gaming house. 'C'mon, boys! The tables and the customers are waiting for you.'

The gamblers walked around the

marshal. They entered the gaming house without looking back at the lawman. Bean touched the brim of his hat, grinned and followed them inside.

Fallen stepped back down into the street. He paced across the width of Front Street and entered Doc's office. Elmer was sitting near the door with the scattergun on his lap.

'Was that them two cardsharps, Marshal?' he asked.

'Yep.' Fallen heaved a sigh. 'Doc in back, Elmer?'

'Sure enough,' Elmer nodded. 'He started cutting Moose open a few minutes back.'

Fallen rested his hands on the window frame and stared out into the street. For a moment he did not speak. Then he glanced at his deputy.

'Did you send a rider to the Lazy D this morning to tell Luke Sutton about what happened to the Brewer boys, Elmer?'

'Yep!' Elmer smiled. 'Just like ya told me. Why?'

'Because Luke and nine of his boys just rode into Front Street, Elmer,' Fallen said.

'Oh glory be!' Elmer jumped out of the chair and pressed his nose up against the window glass. 'And them gamblers ain't left town.'

Luke Sutton led the line of Lazy D cowboys along the wide street. Each of the riders held a cocked rifle in his free hand as he steered his mount.

Fallen opened the door and stepped out onto the porch. Sutton turned the head of his horse and pulled back on its reins. His riders flanked him like the leaves on a tree.

'We come to see ya, Marshal. I got me a bone to pick with ya. We come to ask ya why three of our boys got cut down and ya let the varmints go free. Well?'

Fallen rubbed his mouth on the back of his hand.

'Howdy, Luke,' he greeted the rancher, and sighed.

9

There was a storm brewing in the remote Nevada town. A storm that might make the brutal nightly slayings appear of little account. War Smoke was like a primed stick of dynamite, ready to explode into a bloodbath at any moment. One wrong word might ignite it. Even the experienced Matt Fallen felt helpless as he faced the angry Lazy D cowboys. He had handled a lot of trouble in his decade as a United States marshal but nothing as menacing as this.

He had always thought that the truth was a virtue by which he must always abide, but now he knew that the truth might be the very thing that would set off the carnage.

He glanced around the street at the people who were going through their habitual routine. Women of various ages were buying bread and supplies as they had always done. Fallen knew that there were far too many innocent people in War Smoke for him to tell Sutton and his Lazy D cowboys where the gamblers were.

If lead started to fly, as he knew it surely would, he did not want to be remembered as the man who started it off. It went against his every instinct but he had to lie and lie well enough to fool the cowboys before him.

'Why did ya let 'em go, Matt? I just can't understand it.' Sutton leaned on his saddle horn with both gloved wrists and stared down at the lawman. 'They killed young Johnny and his brothers. Damn it! Ya should have killed them for us.'

Fallen nodded and rubbed his jawline with finger and thumb as his mind raced.

'I reckon you're dead right, Luke. I could have killed them for you,' he agreed.

Luke Sutton looked at his men and

then back at the tall marshal. His head tilted beneath the battered, sweat-stained hat.

'Huh? What ya trying to say, Matt?'

'I agree with you, Luke. I made a mistake. I should have killed those two gamblers, but they had witnesses who said your boys drew on them first.' Fallen looked at the sand as he spoke. 'They claimed it was self-defence.'

Sutton leaned over the neck of his mount. 'Sound like a couple of fancy-talking dudes to me.'

Fallen looked Sutton straight in the eye. 'They are real fancy-talking dudes, Luke.'

'Which way did they go?' Sutton asked. 'Ya gotta be allowed to tell us that.'

Fallen looked along the street. 'I heard tell that they were saying that they were headed for Virginia City, Luke.'

'How much of a start do they have?' one of the other riders asked as he toyed with his saddle rope.

'Not too much of a start.'

'Good. That means they have to head on up through the mountains,' another of the Lazy D cowboys said.

'Yeah!' Sutton nodded firmly. 'And we can head them off if'n we rides through Cooper's Creek and crosses the old river up there.'

'Plenty of stout trees up there with branches just made for hangin',' Fallen said.

'And we're packin' our best ropes, Matt.'

Fallen took a deep breath. 'That's a hard ride, though.'

'Not for Lazy D riders, it ain't.' Luke Sutton dragged his reins hard to his left, turned his horse and spurred. The animal reared and then drove on. With the rest of his men hot on his dust, the rancher thundered back down Front Street and disappeared from view into the afternoon heat haze.

Fallen stepped down to the street, scooped water from the trough and rubbed it over his face and neck.

Elmer walked out on to the board-walk. 'How much time do ya reckon it'll take before Luke and his boys figure out ya lied to them, Marshal?'

Fallen shook his head. Beads of water dropped from his anxious features. He glanced at the deputy.

'Not long enough, Elmer.'

10

Darkness came to War Smoke like a bitter enemy. Fear now swept like a brush fire through the hearts and souls of the town's occupants as one street lantern after another was lit. Even though light also shone out from the windows and doorways of all the stores in the maze of streets besides those of Front Street not one female or child was to be seen. Matt Fallen knew that the men who still braved the unknown killer and walked from one saloon to another, as well as the gaming halls, did so in far fewer numbers than was usual. Those who did venture along the boardwalks carried guns, rifles and even knives.

None of them was taking any undue risks.

Fear had a way of making even the bravest of men appear like cowards. The tall marshal rested his hands on the doorframe to either side of him and stared out into the still warm street. He checked his Colt, then plucked a rifle from the wall stand and cranked its mechanism. It was fully loaded. He slid the Winchester under his left arm and put his Stetson on.

Fallen stepped out into the street and closed the door behind him just as he heard the sound of a solitary horse walking down the almost empty thoroughfare. Fallen turned and screwed up his eyes to view the rider. It was the rancher Bruno Jackson. He was alone and seemingly in no hurry.

Fallen stepped off the boardwalk as Jackson eased his reins back and stopped his horse beside the lawman.

'Jackson.'

'Marshal.'

With the ritual greetings over, Fallen rested his right hand on the horse's neck. He noticed that it had not been ridden hard: there was no hint of its having broken sweat on its journey from the Bar Q.

Fallen looked up at the rancher. The orange light from the numerous lanterns bathed over the owner of the Bar Q.

'I thought you'd be here sooner, Jackson.'

'Why?'

'Ain't you heard about your boy being shot?' Fallen asked the rancher. 'He's bin fighting for his life in Doc Weaver's.'

'I heard but Moose ain't my boy, Marshal,' Jackson said in a way that confused the lawman. 'He's just hired help. Bigger and stronger than most but just hired help all the same.'

Fallen found the words cold. 'But you raised him for the last twenty years or more out on the Bar Q.'

'Still don't make the moron kinfolk, Marshal,' Jackson replied. 'How's the horse?'

Matt Fallen lowered his arm and rested his hand on his gun grip. 'Dead.'

Jackson shook his head. 'Shame. That

was a good horse in its day, Marshal. I only give it to Moose a week or so back. I knew it was a mistake.'

'You ain't even asked how Moose is doing, Jackson,' Fallen said sternly. 'You seem more concerned about that old nag.'

Jackson looked down. 'He ain't dead. Ya already told me that.'

'Yep, I told you that.'

'Reckon this'll cost me a lot of money.' Jackson shook his head. 'Doc Weaver is a sly old fox. I tell ya now, Marshal, I ain't figurin' on paying no bill if it's too high.'

'I'll tell Doc.'

'You do that.'

Fallen went to walk away when another thought struck him. 'You interested in how Moose got shot, Bruno?'

'OK! What happened?' Jackson rolled his eyes. 'Did one of them worthless nesters shoot him?'

'Nope. A bounty hunter picked him and the horse off from one of the rooftops,' Fallen answered.

Jackson shrugged. 'Where's this bounty hunter now?'

'On his way to Boot Hill,' Fallen said bluntly.

'What he shoot Moose for?' Jackson started to smile. 'He think that idiot was an outlaw?'

'Seems that way,' Fallen responded. 'I didn't get a chance to ask him.'

'How come?'

'Because I killed him, Jackson.'

Bruno Jackson pulled out his pocket watch and opened its gold cover. He tilted it until he could see the hands, then returned the timepiece to his pocket. He yawned.

'I gotta go,' he said.

'Moose is in Doc Weaver's back parlour,' Fallen informed the wealthy rancher.

'I got me some important business at the Red Dog.' Jackson tapped his spurs against the side of his horse and the large creature started to walk once more. 'Nice talking to ya.'

Fallen watched as the horseman rode slowly past the Doc's office and on towards the saloon. He rubbed his neck. He had heard rumours that Jackson treated the young man little better than a slave but until this very moment he had not believed it. Now he could see the truth for himself.

'Sorry I bothered you,' Fallen muttered.

The marshal gave the quiet street a long look. He had never seen it this deserted before. He was not sure whether he cared for that or not.

'Marshal?' Elmer's voice broke through Fallen's thoughts.

The lawman turned and looked at his deputy standing under the porch overhang outside Doc's place.

'What, Elmer?'

'Ya want I should do ya rounds with ya, Marshal?' Elmer asked. 'I don't think anyone is gonna try anything with Moose, not with Doc guarding him.'

Matt Fallen strode to the deputy. He

chewed on his lip for a few seconds, then nodded.

'Yeah. Reckon nobody is gonna bother Moose.'

Elmer closed the door of the Doc's office and stepped down to the sand beside Fallen. He still had his scatter-gun in his hands.

'Do ya think we could call into the café before we start patrolling so I can get me a bite to eat, Marshal?'

Fallen started to walk. 'Couple of steaks with biscuits and gravy will keep the night chill out of our bones, Elmer.'

'I ain't got enough for steak, Marshal.'

'My call,' Fallen said.

11

The interior of the Red Dog saloon was unlike the rest of the saloons in War Smoke. Highly polished wooden floors had carpets instead of sawdust covering their surfaces. It had a style which would not have seemed out of place back East in the plushest of bars. It had been among the first saloons to be built when the town was filled with the gold-miners on their way back from California forty years earlier. It reflected a more luxurious time in the town's history.

The whiskey still flowed, though, and the bargirls were still the prettiest, and they still entertained. The Red Dog remained the best.

That was all that counted to the patrons who were willing to pay a little more for their hard liquor as long as the female company was right.

But the fear of the unknown killer

who stalked War Smoke during the hours of darkness had even slowed down the Red Dog's usually thriving trade. There were barely fifteen men inside the large saloon. Most were upstairs being entertained, leaving only four men drinking in the bar.

Jackson drew his mount up outside the saloon and sat for a few moments. At the saloon's four hitching rails, which were usually crowded with horses, only a grey mare stood waiting for its master.

The rancher dismounted, looped his reins over a hitching pole and secured the long leathers. It had not occurred to him until then that the town appeared to be practically empty.

Jackson stepped up on to the boardwalk and entered through the brightly painted double doors. Two steps in and he paused once more. He inhaled the smell of stale perfume and tobacco and purposefully walked across the ornate lobby towards a wall of red drapes through which an archway led into the bar room itself.

He had a thirst after the long ride from his ranch but he also had a curiosity that gnawed at his craw. That was the only reason he was in War Smoke. Curiosity.

The messenger who had brought the news of Moose being gunned down had also delivered a letter from someone Jackson had never heard of. The contents of the letter had piqued the curiosity of the owner of the Bar Q.

It was not what it said, but what it implied.

He glanced around the plush decoration and then headed to the long bar. Jackson was surprised by the fact that the room was almost empty. He rested his right hand on the well-polished surface of the counter and nodded to the bartender.

'Evening, Mr Jackson,' the bartender said. 'Welcome to the Red Dog. Real nice evening.'

'Cut the blarney, Pete,' Jackson snapped.

'Ya usual poison?'

'Yep.'

A shot glass of whiskey was placed before him. Jackson sensed that someone was moving towards him from his blind side.

'You Bruno Jackson?' The voice was low and unfamiliar. It was also Texan.

Jackson held his drink in his hand and turned. He felt his heart quicken at the sight of the tall, spare figure standing there in his trail gear. The man looked out of place in the luxurious surroundings of the Red Dog but there was no one who was foolhardy enough to mention it to Hudson Parker.

'You Parker?' Jackson asked as he sipped at the whiskey.

'Yep,' Parker nodded and pushed his trail coat back over his gun grips. He saw the rancher's eyes lower as they studied the magnificent shooting rig. 'Ya like my guns?'

Jackson nodded slowly. 'Can ya use them?'

'Damn right!'

The Bar Q rancher gestured to a table in a corner. They both walked to it and sat down near the wall. Jackson had never seen anyone quite as menacing as Parker before and he had seen a lot of gunfighters in his time.

'Why did ya write to me, Parker?'

Hudson Parker smiled. It was a cruel smile which had no humour in it. He moved his chair until his back was against the wall and he had a clear, uninterrupted view of the room.

'I thought I made that clear in my note.'

Jackson placed his glass on the table and pulled the letter from his coat pocket. He unfolded it and looked at the grim-faced Parker.

'A man has to read between the lines,' Jackson said. 'I think I understand it, though.'

Parker nodded. 'That's right. It don't pay to put words on paper telling anyone that you'll kill for the right price, Jackson.'

'Smart.'

'Ya don't live too long in my business if ya dumb.'

Jackson signalled to the bartender. His sign language was understood and a bottle of whiskey and another glass was brought to the table. Both men waited until the bartender had returned to his counter.

'How'd ya know that I was looking for a gunfighter?'

Parker smiled. 'I've read how things are getting tense up here between the ranchers and all them farmers who like to fence off the range.'

'That don't answer my question,' the rancher said.

'Ya well known down in Texas, Jackson,' Parker stated. 'A man called Chisum give me ya name and told me all about ya.'

Jackson was thoughtful. 'You'll kill anyone?'

'For a price,' Parker confirmed.

'And that price is?' The rancher downed his whiskey, then opened the bottle and poured out two full measures of the amber liquor. He handed one to the gunfighter, with a tentative smile.

'Depends on who ya wanna have killed.' Parker swallowed his whiskey in one go, then placed the glass next to the bottle. 'The price varies. I heard tell that them farmers have bin giving all the ranchers who use the range a bad time. I'd kill them for a hundred bucks each.'

Jackson held his glass in his hand and studied its contents carefully. His eyes never drifted to the man next to him.

'I'd have sorted them out myself long ago if it weren't for one real righteous man.'

Hudson Parker refilled his glass. 'Fallen?'

At last Jackson looked Parker straight in the eyes. 'You heard of Fallen?'

'Yep.'

'That man has cursed me and my fellow ranchers for ten years now,' Jackson growled. 'He's one of them folks who lives by the rule of law. Before he was made marshal we handled things our own way, but not now. Fallen is a damn curse to us ranchers.'

'Ya mean that Fallen is honest?' Parker nodded. 'That's the worst kinda lawman there is.'

Bruno Jackson rested an elbow on the table. He stared at the man who carried his brutality in every sinew of his being.

'He's like an oak tree. He won't bend.'

'I can get him out of ya hair for good.' Parker downed another whiskey.

'If he was taken out of the picture, things would be a lot easier for me.' Jackson drained his whiskey and slammed his glass down. 'Then I could wipe them farmin' bastards off the face of the earth. Free up the range to our steers again.'

Parker nodded. 'I'll kill Fallen for a thousand bucks, Jackson. In gold coin.'

Once again Jackson looked straight into the eyes of the gunfighter.

'Ya gotta deal, Mr Parker.'

'I want half now and the rest after I deliver.'

'But the banks ain't open until

tomorrow morning.'

'Then stay in town until then.'

Bruno Jackson rubbed his chin with his hand then nodded to himself. He had waited a long time to find someone who was brave enough to take on Fallen. He rose to his feet.

'OK. I'll get me a room over in the High Top for the night, Parker. Meet me outside the bank at ten in the morning.'

'Ten.' Parker repeated the time.

★ ★ ★

Fallen cut a slice of steak and popped it into his mouth as he watched his deputy polishing off the food before him with a sense of awe. He still had a third of his steak remaining on his plate but Elmer was down to the china as he mopped up the last of the gravy with a bread crust.

'You were hungry, Elmer,' Fallen said wryly.

'Still am a tad hungry, Marshal.'

Fallen raised a finger to the cook and caught the man's attention. 'Two slices of pie.'

Elmer smiled wide.

'Do ya figure we'll catch this killer tonight?'

Fallen chewed and nodded. 'I sure hope so.'

Elmer watched as the cook brought two more plates to them with fresh-baked apple pie on them.

'Thank ya kindly,' Elmer said.

As the deputy started to tuck in again, Fallen leaned against the back of his chair and sighed as he wondered about who could be killing so many people. It was a question which refused to leave his tired mind.

'For someone who can put so much grub away you are the thinnest man I've ever seen, Elmer.'

'Miss Peggy from Red Dog says I'm the most active man she ever did know,' Elmer said between mouthfuls. 'She reckons that's why I burn off all the food I eat.'

'She the bargirl with teeth?'

Elmer nodded. 'That's the one.'

'How does she know that?'

Elmer paused. He blushed. 'A gentleman can't answer questions like that when it concerns a lady, Marshal.'

Fallen pushed his own slice of pie toward his deputy. 'Eat that. I'd hate for you to run out of steam. We might run into Miss Peggy.'

Elmer glanced at the wall clock behind the marshal. 'It's nearly six, Marshal.'

Matt Fallen nodded. 'Still early. No point in fretting just yet. The killing don't seem to start until after midnight.'

'I weren't thinkin' of the killer, I was thinking about them Lazy D cowpokes, Marshal,' Elmer corrected. 'Do ya think they've figured out that ya lied to them yet? I ain't relishing them coming back here.'

Fallen picked up a toothpick from the table and started to dig out meat from between his teeth. 'Me neither.

Sutton ain't known for his sense of humour.'

The marshal pulled out two coins from his vest pocket and placed them on the table. Suddenly the muffled sound of gunfire filled the ears of both lawmen and the cook.

'That was shots, Marshal!' the cook exclaimed.

Both Fallen and Elmer jumped to their feet and grabbed their rifles from the floor. They moved swiftly across the café to the door. The marshal opened it, stood in the gentle breeze and listened. Another shot rang out to their left.

'That come from the direction of the livery stable, Marshal.' Elmer pointed the barrel of his scattergun.

'C'mon Elmer!' Fallen raced down the board-walk towards the corner.

12

The lawmen had been wrong. The gunfire had not emanated from the livery stables but from a small lane at the rear of the gaming house known as The Dice. The acrid aroma of outhouses filled the narrow confines of the alleyways but neither marshal nor deputy had time to notice. As both men raced out into the lane from the mean confines of the alley and found themselves caught in the flickering light of a solitary lantern perched on a high pole at the edge of the pathway, the sound of bullets rang out again like thunderclaps. The very end of the wooden fencing shattered as .45 shells tore into them. Sawdust spewed over both Fallen and his stunned follower. Both lawmen instinctively fell to their knees. Fallen pulled himself back as another two bullets cut down through the darkness like crazed fireflies and kicked up sand from the very ground they knelt upon.

'Marshal!' Elmer called out. 'Ya hit?'

'Nope! Not yet anyway!'

Fallen pushed Elmer back behind the weathered timber fence and stared up into the blackness. The moon did not reach the rear of these wood-and-brick structures.

'Where is he?' Elmer asked as he clutched on to his hefty firearm and tried to see over the shoulder of his friend. 'Can ya see him?'

'Not yet,' Fallen replied. 'But he's up high OK.'

Both men could hear movement. Whoever was firing at them was moving. Moving from one building to the next.

'Hear that?'

'Sure enough, Marshal,' Elmer nodded. 'Whoever that is, he ain't wearing spurs.'

'That he ain't, Elmer.'

'Must be a local critter.'

'Figure you're right.' Fallen took a

106

deep breath. 'Cover me!'

There was no time for the deputy to reply. The marshal dropped his Winchester beside Elmer and raced up into the dark alley.

With an agility that he had thought to have long deserted him, Fallen leapt up and caught the top of the fencing. He dragged himself over and dropped down into the yard of one of the buildings. He rushed to the back of the tall wooden structure just as another shot whistled down through the blackness. Fallen pushed himself up against the wall as another bullet hit the ground.

'I see you,' Fallen muttered to himself. The tell-tale red taper line of the bullet had come from the rooftop of the gaming house. The marshal drew his Colt, cocked its hammer and returned two bullets. He could see the sniper against the stars as he moved away from the very edge of the building's rooftop. The lawman holstered his weapon again and climbed up the side of the building until he found something to grip above him. He used every ounce of his strength to haul himself up until he could swing his right leg on to the balcony overhead.

He rested for a few seconds. His eyes were slowly adjusting to the shadows. Then he saw the man move once more. Whoever it was jumped down from the top of The Dice onto the roof of the café.

Fallen stepped on to the wooden rail and leapt. His hands caught the edge of the roof of The Dice. The marshal dragged himself on to the shingles and clawed his way up, away from the twenty-foot drop. The man who had shot at them was making a lot of noise as he tried to find a way down from the café. Fallen knew he had no time to waste.

Forcing himself up on to his feet, Fallen ignored his fears. He ran across the slanted roof until he reached the point from where he had seen the man leap. Fallen did not pause. He kept running and vaulted across the distance between the two buildings.

He hit the café roof hard. He staggered and fell on to his face just as a shot was fired. Fallen felt the heat of the lead as it cut through his shirtsleeve and grazed his arm. He buckled for a second, then drew his Colt once more.

Again he fired. Again his target had gone.

Fallen crawled towards where he had last seen the man's elusive outline against the backdrop of a million stars. Yet again the gunman was gone.

Suddenly to his left he heard the sound of boots hitting a porch overhang. Then the softer thud as the man landed on the sand of Front Street. Fallen rose with his gun in his hand and raced to the façade above Front Street. He leaned over and could hear the noise of a man running along the boardwalks away from him. Desperately his eyes searched as he held the deadly gun in his right hand.

'Damn it!' Fallen cursed.

The gunman had disappeared like a phantom into the night. Slowly Fallen's thumb lowered the cocked hammer. He dropped the Colt into his holster and looked around for an easier way back down to the ground than the one which had got him to where he was.

After a few minutes Fallen had managed to get down from the café roof. He walked back at pace to where he had left his deputy. Elmer stood holding both rifles in his arms beside the high fencing as the marshal came to a halt beside him.

'Ya got yaself winged, Marshal!' There was concern in Elmer's voice. 'Best we get ya over to Doc's.'

'Look at my hand, Elmer.' Fallen showed the palm of his left hand under the lantern. The younger man placed the rifles up against the fence and looked close.

'Blood,' Elmer said. 'But ya have bin winged, Marshal.'

'This ain't my blood!' Fallen corrected. 'I landed in it up on the top of the café! This is the shooter's blood!'

'Ya managed to shoot him.'

Fallen shook his head. 'Nope. My shots never got close to him.'

Elmer looked confused. 'Ya got me kinda baffled here, Marshal. If'n it weren't you, then who did shoot that bushwhacking *hombre?* And why?'

'I wonder.' The marshal turned and stared into the shadows. He walked away from his panting deputy and looked hard into the darkness between two buildings. He looked at Elmer and nodded to himself. 'Think about it. The so called maniac killer has struck silently each time, Elmer.'

'Right enough.'

'Then if this was the man we've bin chasing, how come a shot was fired? It don't fit the pattern.'

'Glory be.' Elmer was excited. 'Ya got something there. It don't make no sense him drawing attention to himself. If the gunman was the maniac, I mean.'

Fallen rubbed the blood off on his pants leg and ventured further into the darkness. Elmer kept level with his every stride until the deputy paused, tapped the arm of the bigger man and pointed.

'Look!'

'What you see, Elmer?'

'Can't ya see it, Marshal?'

Matt Fallen screwed up his eyes. He saw it OK.

'Oh yeah! I see it!' Fallen walked forward towards the boots protruding from behind the large garbage barrel. Fallen pulled out a box of matches from his vest pocket, leaned over and struck one. He held its flame above the brutalized head of the victim. 'By the looks of this battered head I'd say it's a fair bet that that was the maniac we just ran off, Elmer.'

'Can ya make out who the victim is, Marshal?'

'Yep,' Fallen answered and tossed the match away. 'The maniac didn't have time to finish this one off like the others.'

Elmer swallowed hard. 'W . . . who is it?'

Fallen grabbed hold of the ankles of both legs. 'You'll see once I get this critter out into the light.'

Elmer cleared his throat. 'I'll help ya.'

Both men hauled the heavy corpse across the soft sand until it was out where the high lantern's light could illuminate it.

'Well, look at that!' Elmer gasped in realization. 'It's the mayor! It's Sol Hancock!'

'Yeah.' Fallen released his grip on the ankles. He stared down at the partially crushed features. 'Our maniac didn't get to complete the job this time.'

Elmer rubbed his neck. 'I wonder why?'

Fallen bent over and plucked a small Remington .38 from the hand of the mayor and held it in the palm of his own.

'This is why.' Fallen raised the gun to his nostrils and inhaled. The barrel was still warm and he could smell the gunsmoke. 'Sol was armed and got a shot off when he was jumped. The killer then started to do his work and must have heard us running down the alley.'

'Otherwise he would have finished the job.'

'Yep.'

The deputy could see the confusion in Fallen's face. 'What's wrong, Marshal?'

The marshal looked down at the face. 'What was Sol doing out here in the middle of the night, Elmer?'

'Maybe he was using the outhouse?'

Fallen nodded and then snapped his fingers. A wry smile etched his features.

'I just had me a thought.'

Elmer drew close. 'What would that be?'

Fallen rubbed a knuckle across his chin. 'The maniac killer is wounded, Elmer. Maybe not badly but wounded all the same.'

'Do ya figure he left a trail of blood out on Front Street, Marshal?'

'There's only one way to find out,' Fallen said. He picked up both rifles and tossed the scattergun to his deputy. 'Let's take us a look.'

13

The bright moon cast its eerie light across the vast tree-covered mountain range and the horsemen who were returning to War Smoke. Luke Sutton led the line of dust-caked Lazy D riders along the narrow track on the downward trail towards the distant settlement. He and his stalwart cowboys were cold and in even worse tempers than when they had left the remote town more than thirteen hours earlier.

Not one of them could work out why they had not encountered the pair of gamblers they wanted to neck-stretch with their sturdy cutting ropes on the trail. None of them even considered the possibility that Matt Fallen had lied to mislead them. To them, there had to be another answer.

Foreman Jonas Pyle was Sutton's oldest cowboy. He had been with

Sutton since the rancher had first branded the Lazy D on to the hides of his cattle. Pyle was a willowy man who seemed to be shrinking as age slowly crept up on him. Yet he had never lost any of his skills or appetite for riding free with no other worries than collecting his monthly pay. Pyle had become like a father to most of the Lazy D cowboys and taught them everything they needed to know to survive the seasons without too many broken bones. It was Pyle who wanted revenge more than most of the others. To him, it had been one or other of the Brewer brothers who would one day fill his boots.

Now he realized that there was really nobody left capable of doing that. Pyle would have to start again and find another successor.

Trip Stone was almost as old as Sutton and Pyle but looked at least a decade younger. He had been blessed with many things including an ability to break any mustang he had ever sat upon in minutes rather than hours. Yet, like Pyle, he wanted to use his rope and hang the men who had brutally slaughtered Johnny, Ike and Dabs.

There was a saying that there was no fury like that of a cowboy when he believed he had been wronged.

There was also another saying.

Never kill a cowboy, for ten more will appear with guns blazing looking for vengeance before the dust settles.

The riders reached the flatter ground and knew that there was now only swaying grass between them and their goal. They could see the lights of War Smoke away in the distance ahead of them and started to spur.

The horses gathered pace.

They were like moths to a naked flame. It was impossible for them to resist the lure. They were being drawn to the place where, unknown to the cowboys, the men they sought remained defiant.

Luke Sutton spurred and leaned over the neck of his gelded sorrel. The

117

rancher had no idea that he was leading the last of the Lazy D riders into the unknown.

Into the jaws of death.

14

The trail of blood droplets had led halfway along Front Street to the corner of the High Top and then vanished. Neither lawman could understand how but knew there was little point in fretting. Their prey had eluded them yet again. To Fallen it was becoming more and more obvious that this was no insane creature he was chasing. Whatever everyone else in War Smoke believed, he knew that there was a rational mind behind all the barbaric acts. No maniac could kill so brutally and still have enough savvy to escape detection for so long.

The marshal knew in his guts that the man they sought was probably someone who looked and acted no differently from anyone else in town.

But if that theory was correct, what was the motive? Even Fallen, with his long ten years of experience, could not answer that question.

After waking up the undertaker and telling him about Sol Hancock's body, the dejected lawmen walked back along Front Street until they reached the marshal's office. They entered silently. As Elmer turned the lamp up to fill the office with light, Fallen sat down behind his desk and tossed his hat across the room angrily.

'Shall I put a fresh pot of coffee on, Marshal?' Elmer asked as he placed the rifles back on the wall stand and chained them securely.

Fallen nodded. 'Might as well. Reckon we'll stay here for an hour or so and then take us another walk around town.'

'But the killer's already struck, Marshal,' Elmer pointed out. 'I don't think he'll bother to kill anyone else tonight.'

'But tonight he seems to be making new rules for himself, Elmer,' Fallen contended.

'Ya seem a tad troubled,' Elmer

observed as he filled the blackened coffee pot with water from a canteen and placed it upon the hot stove top.

'Something's real wrong,' Fallen said thoughtfully, looking at his hands. 'Something's this close to my nose and I can't see it, Elmer.'

'Sure there's something wrong.' Elmer smiled as he poured ground coffee into the pot and closed its lid. 'Another critter got hisself killed tonight by the maniac.'

The marshal rubbed his chin. 'No, there's something else bothering me, but for the life of me I just can't figure out what.'

'Ya just worn out, Marshal.' Elmer moved to the law officer's side and touched the torn, blood-stained shirtsleeve. 'Ya really ought to go to let Doc take a look at that ya know.'

'Doc's got enough on his plate tending to young Moose.'

Elmer sounded like a mother hen. 'Now ya shouldn't go on like that. Doc'll tend ya just fine if'n ya let him.'

Fallen shook his head. 'Think about

what just happened, Elmer. Think about it and see if all the pieces fit the puzzle.'

Elmer raised his eyebrows. 'What puzzle would that be, Marshal?'

The marshal sighed heavily. 'Why would the killer change his pattern? Why would he?'

'We already talked about that!' Elmer said. 'Sol managed to get a shot off and wing him before he could crush the mayor's skull. If Sol hadn't had a gun on him he'd have had his head caved in just like all the others.'

Fallen stood. 'Not that. Why did he kill so early? All the other murders happened after midnight. Why did he change his pattern? Why?'

'Ya gotta be loco to be able to work that out, Marshal.'

The marshal shook his head again and paced the floor of the room, mumbling to himself. Then he paused by the stove and stared at the deputy long and hard.

'What if the killer is sane, Elmer? I've bin thinking that for the last couple of days now. What if he just wants us to think he's loco?'

Elmer chuckled. 'Now ya just joshin' with me. No sane man goes around smashing people's heads to pulp.'

'He would if there was another reason behind the killings,' Fallen stated firmly. 'Where's the list of all the people that's bin killed, Elmer?'

The deputy tutted, picked up the sheet of paper from the desk and waved it at his superior. 'Here it is, but what's looking at all them names again gonna do?'

Matt Fallen grabbed the paper and sat down again. His eyes raced over the pencil scribbling. He read each name silently, then he smiled.

'What ya smiling for, Marshal?'

Fallen looked at Elmer.

'I think I might have figured this out.'

★ ★ ★

Maybe it was the echoing sound of gunshots which had woken the youngster up from his deep enforced sleep.

Perhaps it was his own physical strength which enabled him to fight his way back into consciousness. Either way, his eyes opened and looked up at the tobacco-stained ceiling above him. For a moment panic filled his heart. Then Moose Coltrane rose from the cot in the back parlour of Doc Weaver's place.

He blinked hard.

A candle burned a few feet away from him. He swung his long powerful legs over the edge of the bed and rested them on the cold floor. He could not understand where this strange, unfamiliar room was. Or why he was here.

Then he saw the small figure sleeping in an armchair near the door, with a pipe dangling from his mouth. Although he had never actually met the doctor, he recognized him.

His mind became aware of the bandages which encircled his chest in several directions. Again he blinked and attempted to get his brain to work and explain what was happening.

It did not work.

Even an undamaged mind would have found the situation beyond its ability to reason.

'You!' Moose said in a low grunt.

The husky tone awoke the doctor. Doc opened his eyes and glanced across at his patient in surprise. He forced his ancient bones up and then shuffled slowly to the confused man.

'Howdy, Moose,' Doc said in a low calming tone. 'You bin a tad ill, son.'

Moose blinked frantically. He was scared.

'You hurt me?'

Doc paused and smiled. 'No, Moose. I helped you after somebody filled you with lead, boy.'

The large blunt fingers touched the bandages. Moose winced when he felt the raw wounds beneath them. His eyes met those of the old man.

'Doc?'

'Yep.'

'Thanks.'

'My pleasure.' Doc was taken back. He had heard that Moose barely spoke and yet the young man seemed able and even willing to communicate.

He placed a hand on the muscular shoulder. 'I thought that you'd be unconscious for at least another day or so. Most folks would have been. But most folks ain't built like you are, boy. I had me a lotta trouble finding them bullets in ya.'

'Doc.' Moose repeated the name and suddenly the smile returned to the big face. 'Doc good.'

The medical man chortled.

'You wanna cup of coffee, boy?' Doc asked. 'Ain't too good but it's hot and black.'

'Water,' Moose said.

Doc nodded and went towards the water jug. Then he paused. He looked at the big man sitting staring at him.

'I bet you've never even tasted hot coffee, have ya?'

Moose shook his head. 'Water.'

Doc handed a tumbler of the clear liquid to his patient and watched as Moose swallowed it fast.

'Good?'

Moose nodded.

Suddenly the sound of riders yelling and firing their guns filled the room. Moose seemed frightened. Doc moved to the window and parted the drapes. He squinted into the lantern-lit street.

'Cowboys! It's just cowboys!'

★ ★ ★

Marshal Fallen was out on to the street with his gun drawn before the Lazy D cowboys had ridden halfway down the wide thoroughfare. Elmer was a few strides behind him with his own .45 cocked and ready for action. Both lawmen walked slowly out across the lantern-lit sand and stared at the riders as they heralded their arrival back in War Smoke with wild reckless gunfire.

'Do ya reckon they might be a tad upset, Marshal?'

'Yep.' Fallen dragged the hammer back on his Colt, raised his arm and fired up into the air. Even above the noise of their own gunplay, the cowboys heard the marshal's shot. The lawmen watched as the cowboys spun their mounts around and saw them.

'Ya got their attention OK,' Elmer whispered.

'Well spotted!' said Fallen drily.

Luke Sutton glared at the two men standing defiantly in the middle of the street. He spurred hard and thundered towards them. The rest of his cowboys were close on the tail of the sorrel.

'I reckon we oughta run, Marshal,' Elmer suggested.

'Stand firm!'

The cowboys hauled rein as they reached the grim-faced lawman and his deputy. Within seconds the horsemen had surrounded both Fallen and Elmer.

Fallen narrowed his eyes as his thumb pulled the hammer of his gun back again until it was fully locked.

'Holster them guns,' the marshal commanded.

None of the Lazy D riders listened. They kept firing in all directions as they circled the two men in the middle of the street.

Fallen looked straight up at Sutton and raised his arm until the long barrel of his weapon was trained on the rancher. 'You heard me, Luke. I ain't gonna argue with you.'

'What ya gonna do, Matt?' Sutton snarled. 'Ya gonna shoot me or something?'

'Yep, I'll put a hole right through you,' came the cold reply.

The cowboys reined back. They all stared down at the marshal with his steady hand holding the pistol at arm's length. Each of them knew that this was no bluff.

Men like Matt Fallen never bluffed.

'Reckon he's serious, Luke,' Jonas Pyle said, dropping his gun into its holster. 'Listen to him.'

The rest of the cowboys nodded in agreement.

Luke Sutton was no fool. He lowered

his gun and stared through the smoke which drifted from its hot barrel.

'Them gamblers never showed, Matt,' Sutton muttered. 'We waited and waited but they never showed.'

'We waited for hours on the Virginia City trail,' Trip Stone added. 'Are ya sure they headed west, Marshal?'

'You said they was headed to Virginia City!' Luke Sutton spat out his words like a rattler's venom.

Fallen lowered his own weapon. 'I said that I heard that they were figurin' on going to Virginia City, boys. I never said that they did.'

The rancher dragged his reins up to his chest and glared at the lawmen below him. He looked at his cowboys and then back at Fallen.

'Ya lied?'

'I just kinda twisted the truth a little, Luke,' Fallen admitted. 'I had no choice.'

'But why?'

'If I'd let you do what you wanted to do I'd have bin forced to arrest all of you for murder.' Fallen slid his Colt into its holster and sighed. 'I don't want to hang any of you.'

For a moment there was nothing but silence on Front Street as both sides mulled over each other's words. The cowboys knew that Fallen followed the rule of law whatever the cost. The marshal knew that he might just have managed to avert a bloodbath.

Sutton pushed his gun back into its holster. He nodded and touched the brim of his battered old hat.

'Ya right, Matt,' he admitted.

Fallen lowered his head. 'Take ya boys back to the Lazy D, Luke. I'll make the arrangements for Johnny and his brothers' funerals.'

'Much obliged.'

Then a sound behind the cowboys drew their attention. They all swung their mounts around and saw the two tinhorn gamblers leaving The Dice.

Jonas Pyle raised a hand and pointed a knowing finger in the direction of Ace Marsden and Dandy Jim Larsen. 'That's the cheatin' critters who cleaned me and the boys out in the War Smoke, Luke!'

Sutton looked at Fallen. 'Is that them, Matt?'

Fallen said nothing.

'It is.' The rancher gritted his teeth and drove his horse straight at the two gamblers, who were making their way towards their hotel.

'We gotta do something, Marshal,' Elmer urged.

Fallen remained silent.

Like the well-trained wranglers they were, the Lazy D cowboys spun their ropes as they had done so often out on the range. This time they were not after the heads of mavericks; they were aiming for the necks of the gamblers.

It was Larsen who turned first as the sound of the hoofs came closer behind him and his partner. The man known as Dandy Jim drew his gun from its concealed holster. Marsden spun on his heels as he heard the chilling sound of ropes flying through the air. He followed Larsen's move and drew his gun from its hiding-place beneath his left arm.

The gamblers started to shoot as rope loops landed all around them. Marsden saw one of his bullets hit a cowpuncher off his saddle as Trip Stone's rope encompassed his shoulders. The cowboy wrapped the end of his cutting rope around his saddle horn and hauled rein. Marsden was pulled off his feet and crashed through a hitching rail.

Larsen blasted his gun at the Lazy D riders. Two of the horsemen fell from their mounts. The gambler went to fire again when another rope wrapped around his arm and was tightened with incredible speed.

Fallen and Elmer moved closer.

'What'll we do, Marshal?'

'We wait,' came the firm reply.

The gamblers were on their backs in the street. Marsden still fired and somehow managed to hit his target. Pyle clutched at his chest and crashed to the sand. Sutton whipped the shoulders of his horse. The animal leapt forward and landed on top of Marsden before he could fire again. The rancher kept whipping his horse as its hoofs pounded down on the stricken gambler.

Dandy Jim Larsen fired up through the dust in which he found himself enveloped, aiming at the cowboys until another rope looped around his neck and tightened. Then two cowboys spurred and dragged Larsen down the street at top flight. By the time they reached the Red Dog there was little left of the gambler.

Then, as quickly as it had started, it was over.

Those who remained of the Lazy D men dismounted and checked their dead and injured. None of them noticed as Fallen and Elmer strolled silently among them to the bodies of the gamblers.

'They're both dead,' Fallen said bluntly.

'What we gonna do, Marshal?' Elmer

asked. 'We gonna arrest Luke and the boys?'

Fallen rested a hand on his deputy's shoulders. 'Nope.'

'We ain't?'

'Self-defence, Elmer.' Fallen gave a sigh. 'Those cardsharps started shooting first. Self-defence. It was good enough for them and I figure it's good enough for Luke and his crew.'

Elmer smiled 'So it were, Marshal. So it were.'

'Go get Doc, Elmer,' Fallen said. 'I reckon his services are needed by some of these rope-twirlers.'

As the deputy ran off in the direction of the doc's office, the tall marshal stopped walking and looked at Luke Sutton, who was kneeling beside one of his fallen men.

Both men nodded to one another.

15

The office clock chimed. It was only ten and the night had another eight hours of darkness ahead of it before dawn. Matt Fallen had silently pondered the list of victims' names since the brutal fight out in Front Street. Then the sound of boots on the boardwalk outside alerted him that someone was heading to the door of his office. He leaned back in his chair and stared at the door as its brass handle turned. Elmer entered and walked towards his desk.

'Well?' Elmer said as he checked the coffee pot. 'Ya figured it out yet?'

'Reckon so,' Fallen said.

Elmer looked impressed. 'I know ya said ya had worked out the connection with all them dead 'uns before Luke and his boys rode into town and started shootin', but I thought ya was funnin' with me, Marshal.'

The marshal stood and brought his empty tin cup to his deputy. He held it as more of the black beverage was poured into it. He then moved across his office and sat on his cot next to the jail cells.

'Well?' Elmer urged.

It was a tired Matt Fallen who looked up at Elmer. 'At first the names seem kinda random. But then I started to try and work out if there was any link between them.'

Elmer filled his own cup, walked to the table and sat down on the safest of the hardback chairs.

'Go on.' He smiled. 'This sounds like it's gonna be exciting, Marshal.'

Fallen stared into the steam rising from the coffee and fought off his weariness. 'It all hinges on Sol Hancock, I reckon.'

Elmer raised his eyebrows. 'He couldn't be the killer. He got his head stove in.'

The marshal smiled. 'I didn't say he

did it, Elmer. I said it all hinges on or around our dead mayor.'

Elmer placed his cup on the table and looked baffled. 'Is ya gonna tell me or not?'

'Think about all those names, Elmer,' Fallen said, his eyes focusing on his deputy. 'At first it was just folks who live in town. Men, women and even kids. Then I noticed the name of Doris Harvey.'

'But she was just a widow woman living on the edge of War Smoke, Marshal,' Elmer retorted. 'I can't see why ya picked her handle out of the bunch.'

'A widow woman who had no money after her husband up and died,' Fallen added.

'I still ain't no wiser.'

'A widow woman who cleaned house for Sol Hancock,' Fallen stressed.

'Keep going.' Elmer scratched his neck hair.

Fallen blew into the cup in his hand. 'She had keys to his house, Elmer.'

'So what?'

'Then a few other murders later we have ourselves a victim called Sam Williams!' Fallen kept looking at the face opposite him. 'Sam was Sol's right-hand man. Sam did everything for our fat mayor. Kept Sol's house running like a well-greased wagon wheel.'

Elmer picked up his cup and took a swallow of the coffee.

'And Sam would have keys to Hancock's place as well.'

Fallen pointed a finger at his deputy. 'Exactly.'

Elmer smiled and then frowned. 'So?'

'I checked with the undertaker when you were out and he told me that neither Doris nor Sam had any keys on them when they were killed, Elmer.'

'But Sol never had his house broken into,' Elmer said.

'Not that we know.' Fallen lifted the cup to his lips and took a sip. He lowered it again. 'How could we tell if a thief used keys to get in and out? If a thief did not disturb anything inside Sol's large house? We've both bin in that barn of a house and seen it for ourselves. Sol had stuff everywhere. The guy was wealthy and filled that house with so much junk that even he would be hard pressed to know if anything went missing.'

Elmer nodded. 'What about Sol's body?'

'No keys.'

'None at all?'

'None at all, Elmer.' Fallen downed the black brew, and then lay on the cot and sighed. 'I reckon someone needed something in Sol's place and the killings were just to muddy the water so nobody would figure out what.'

Elmer got up and walked to the cot. He looked down at the marshal.

'Maybe we oughta go and take us a look at Sol's house for ourselves, Marshal.'

'After I've had me some shut-eye.' Fallen sighed again. 'I'm so tuckered that my brain ain't working any more.'

Elmer shook his head and stared into his cup. 'Reckon I'll make a fresh pot. This stuff tastes like Doc's so-called coffee.'

Without warning, the door of the office burst open and Doc stood there, panting like an old hound dog after a vain attempt to catch a fox. Fallen rose up from the cot and looked at the troubled old man.

'What's wrong, Doc?'

'It's Moose, Matt!' Doc said. 'He's gone!'

'What?' Fallen forced his tired frame up off the cot. He walked to the medical man. 'I don't understand.'

'He got spooked when them wounded cowboys was brought to my office, Matt. He just lit out like his tail was on fire!'

Fallen stepped out into the lantern-lit street and bent over the trough. He cupped his hands together, scooped water out and splashed it over his face and neck. Rising again to his full height he accepted his hat from Elmer. After running wet fingers through his dark

141

hair he placed the Stetson on his head and gritted his teeth.

'He couldn't have gone far, Doc,' Fallen said as his eyes searched Front Street vainly for a clue. 'Not after having a couple of bullets dug out of him.'

'That boy is as strong as an ox but I'm feared his stitches will bust open,' Doc said anxiously. 'If that happens he'll be dead in a matter of minutes.'

Fallen looked at his deputy. 'C'mon, Elmer! Let's try and find that youngster!'

'But ya plumb worn out, Marshal,' Elmer protested.

Fallen smiled. 'There ain't no rest for the wicked.'

16

The large moon was almost directly above the big wooden livery and cast its haunting light down over the stable and its adjoining corral. Clem Doyle heard someone moving clumsily below his hayloft. The liveryman struggled to his feet from the place where he had lain down a few hours earlier and walked to the window situated above the locked doors to his stable building.

He rested a hand on the pulley used to haul up bales of hay and stared down at the figure below his lofty perch.

The large young man was barefoot. He also seemed dazed and was pounding on the secured stable doors without apparently knowing why. Perhaps, in his weakened state, Moose Coltrane had sought and found a place similar to the one in which he had spent the previous twenty years of his life on the Bar Q ranch.

Whatever the reason, his large fists continued to pound on the tall doors pitifully.

Doyle narrowed his eyes in disbelief. He recognized the figure but could not believe that anyone who had been so severely wounded only half a day earlier would be capable of standing, let alone walking to his workplace from Doc Weaver's.

The news of the shooting had reached him only minutes after it had happened, by word of mouth. He continued looking down at the lumbering Moose in amazement. It seemed impossible that anyone could be so powerful after undergoing surgery. If it were not for the bandages that were wrapped around the distressed Moose's huge torso, Doyle might not have believed the report of the shooting was true. But the bandages bore evidence.

'Is that you, Moose?' Doyle called down.

Moose paused, looked up and nodded. 'Moose.'

'What in tarnation are ya doing?'

'Moose tired. Want sleep.'

Doyle had deliberately locked his stable doors with a hefty plank of wood across their width. There was no way that he wished to discover another body in his stables, as he had done the previous morning. But as his doors swayed on their hinges he knew that eventually they would succumb to the strength of the troubled youth.

'Git going, Moose!' he ordered.

Moose looked towards the voice. Moonlight caught the pitiable expression. The youngster fell to his knees. He was worn out by the confused walk through the dark alleys that had led him to this place. He shook his head and tried to shake the fog that clouded his already fragile mind.

It did not work.

'Sleep,' Moose mumbled and fell on to his back. His left arm rose and a finger pointed upward at Doyle. 'I sleep.'

'Damn it all!' Clem Doyle cursed and

swallowed hard. He knew that whatever Moose was, he was no killer. The liveryman went to the wooden ladder and climbed down to the floor of the livery stable.

Doyle moved across the dirt to the doors. He removed the long plank from its iron brackets and pushed the doors open.

'What the hell are ya doing here?' Doyle asked as he bent over the gasping Moose. 'Ya ought to be at Doc's, not here.'

'Sorry,' Moose muttered.

'Come here, boy!' Clem Doyle carefully put his own powerful arms around the chest of youth who was now lapsing into delirium. During nearly forty years as a blacksmith Doyle had forged not only horseshoes but muscles made of iron. He hauled the huge Moose off the sand and then balanced him against his own sweat-covered shoulder. He scooped a hand under the left armpit of the weakened young man. 'Don't fret none! I gotcha!'

Slowly they moved back towards the dark interior of the cavernous building.

Doyle had lifted many things in his time but nothing quite as challenging as Moose.

Suddenly the liveryman heard something behind him. He tried to turn and see but with Moose leaning on him, it was impossible.

'Who is it?' Doyle asked through gritted teeth.

There was no verbal answer.

Only the grip of a handgun as it crashed down on the back of his skull replied. Doyle buckled but somehow managed to ease his burden down before another mighty blow smashed across his head.

Clem Doyle hit the ground beside the unconscious Moose. He forced himself over on to his side and stared through the blood that poured like a red waterfall from the brutal gashes on his head.

He saw the man with the gun in his hand.

'Who are ya?'

The gun came down again in bitter reply. This time with more force.

Clem Doyle was dead.

17

Ferocious flames leapt up into the black night sky. Red, twisting rods of lethal energy intent on burning the very stars and moon above shot upward in their fury. The hideous sound of horses trapped inside the burning building could be heard all over War Smoke as men raced from every direction with buckets in hands. But it was too late to do anything except dampen the surrounding wooden buildings against the showers of burning embers which floated like a million fireflies from what remained of the once proud livery stable.

Fallen and Elmer had been on the opposite side of town when the flames first cut up into the black sky. They had raced for all they were worth to the place where men had already started to battle against the hot, cruel enemy.

The two lawmen stood watching as others pumped water and tried to extinguish the inferno. The pair of bodies which had been found outside the wide-open doors of the stable had been dragged to where Fallen and his deputy stood. They lay lifeless at the lawmen's feet.

Even though Doyle's face was unrecognizable the unmistakable contours of his body told Fallen and Elmer whom they were looking down upon. The body of Moose was a different matter, though. He lay untouched by the merciless gun grip of the deadly killer. He lay with his face looking with eyes that could no longer see up into the sky.

'He's still smiling, Marshal,' Elmer said in a low hushed tone. 'Still smiling.'

Fallen swallowed. 'Yep.'

'How come the killer didn't stove Moose's face in like he done to old Clem?'

'I don't know, Elmer.' Fallen turned his eyes away from the hideous sight and focused on the blazing stables again. 'Maybe we'll never know.'

There was little remaining of what had only minutes earlier been the largest building in War Smoke. Blackened wood, flames and smoke marked the scorched earth on the sandy ground.

Fallen knew that this destruction was more than likely deliberate. But he did not know why the killer had chosen now to set fire to the livery stable.

'How come he didn't burn this place down yesterday, Elmer?'

'How do ya know the killer did this, Marshal?'

'Smell that air,' Fallen said. 'Kerosene. I got a feeling in my craw that this is just a way to sidetrack us.'

The deputy shuffled away from the marshal to stand closer to the flames and those who were vainly battling against them. The heat was so intense he could feel his skin scorching. He edged back.

'Gotta be a locobean that done this.'

Fallen shook his head. 'I don't think so.'

'But look at Clem, Marshal. No normal man would up and do that.'

'I figure that a real normal man is behind this,' Fallen argued. 'Maybe he ain't doing the killing but he's guiding the one who is.'

'How can ya say that?'

Matt Fallen pointed at the ground between them and the men who were running back and forth from troughs with buckets of water.

'What do you see, Elmer? Tell me what you see.'

'Just churned-up sand,' Elmer answered.

Fallen grabbed his deputy by the elbow, steered him to his left and pointed down at two deep grooves in the sand. Two grooves that led from the stable off into the lanes.

'See them tracks?'

'Sure enough,' Elmer replied. 'Them's just wagon tracks. So what?'

'Somebody took a wagon from the livery, Elmer,' Fallen said firmly. 'Hitched up a pair of horses and drove off.'

'Are ya sure?' Elmer asked. 'Them tracks might have bin there for the longest time.'

Fallen shook his head.

'They weren't there when I patrolled earlier,' Fallen said. 'And the wagon was inside at the back of the stables. Nope, someone hitched it up and took it.'

Elmer looked confused. 'What for?'

'That's what I was wondering, Elmer,' Fallen said. 'Why take a wagon? What would anyone need a wagon for?'

'To move something heavy like, I guess.'

'Yeah.' Fallen pondered the thought. 'Something heavy!' Elmer rubbed his sweat-soaked hair off his face. 'Kinda confusing, though.'

Marshal Fallen gave the two bodies a sad glance, then started to walk away from the horrific scene of murder and destruction with his deputy at his side.

'Where we going, Marshal?'

'C'mon, Elmer. Maybe if we follow the trail left by them wagon tracks we'll finally have us an answer.'

★ ★ ★

Outlaw Texas Tom McCree sat and waited in the shadows of the Golden Garter saloon. He pulled the cork from a whiskey bottle with his teeth and spat it across the sawdust-covered floor. He took a long swallow, and then placed the bottle of amber liquor down on the floor beside his left leg. Without uttering a word he drew his handgun from its holster and inspected it.

There could be few sights more sickening than that of human gore and drying bloodied scalp hair on the grip of a six-shooter, yet McCree never batted an eyelid. He had sunk to a depth of depravity few men would have thought possible. He wallowed in his own filth and that of those who paid him without a single regret. Perhaps all that could be said of him in mitigation was that he might do what others wanted but it was in their twisted minds that the original thoughts were created. He was simply the person willing to put

153

into effect the hideous imaginings.

McCree stared at the grip of the weapon: the weapon he had used to bludgeon so many people to death. McCree pulled his bandanna loose from his neck and began to clean the gun methodically, as he had done so many times before during the short period of time he had been in War Smoke. No butcher could have left his tools more pristine than McCree left his gun.

When satisfied he dropped it back into his holster and scooped up the bottle once more.

The outlaw had been in town for more than two weeks but no one had set eyes upon him except the cunning man who had hired him in the first place. A man to whom few in War Smoke ever gave a second look.

McCree sat and drank and watched.

Some of his victims had caught a brief glimpse of him a fraction of a heartbeat before he had permanently ended their existences. Most had gone to their maker never knowing who had killed them. Either way it meant nothing to the hardened outlaw.

McCree stared, with eyes devoid of any emotion, long and hard across the saloon at the man who had brought him north to this place.

'Ya happy now?' the outlaw asked.

'Ya brought the wagon like I told ya?' a voice responded as the man moved across the dark bar room towards McCree.

McCree nodded.

'Yep. It's tied up out back in the yard.'

'Good.'

'I still don't get why ya had me kill all them folks!' McCree muttered. 'It don't figure none!'

The sound of laughter filled the empty saloon.

'That's the point, Texas Tom. It don't make no sense at all unless ya know what I know.'

McCree stared at his paymaster. 'When do I get paid for all the work

I've done, Jones?'

'Tonight. When we finish the job.' Barkeep Hec Jones struck a match and lit a cigar. He blew smoke at the floor, then lit the wick of a candle on the end of the bar. The flickering light played upon the faces of the incongrous pair.

McCree rose to his feet and moved close to the smaller man, who was pouring himself a whiskey at the bar.

'Ya got mighty big plans for a little runt, Jones.'

'I might be small but I've got me the keys to something that'll make us both richer than we could ever have dreamed, Texas,' Jones said.

'Thanks to me,' McCree said bluntly. 'Reckon it was ya lucky day when I bumped into ya brother down in Houston.'

Jones pulled out the keys McCree had taken from three of his victims and waved them under the nose of the outlaw.

'Ya know what these keys unlock, Texas Tom?'

McCree shook his head. 'The bank?'

'Nope. They unlock something far more profitable.' Jones downed his whiskey and refilled his glass.

The outlaw looked at the man who had hired him. 'What could be more profitable than a bank, Jones?'

Hec Jones looked at McCree. 'Listen up! I used to work for the fat, lazy bastard Sol Hancock until he got fancy and wanted folks in suits around instead of me. I was with him for years and I knew as much about him as he knew about himself. The man was a thief. He stole thousands from every business deal he ever had anything to do with. He also milked the local town council. But he never put much faith in banks. Banks get robbed. Hancock wanted to hold on to his ill-gotten gains. These are the keys to Hancock's house and the secret vault he had built into it.'

McCree suddenly looked impressed.

'Vault? The kind with money in, ya mean?'

'Paper money and silver and gold coin, Texas Tom.' Jones smiled. 'Only I know where it is inside that castle of a home Hancock built himself. Ya killed the only two other folks who knew the secret! Apart from yours truly, nobody has any idea of its existence, let alone where it is.'

Texas Tom McCree inhaled deeply. 'When we gonna go empty that vault, Jones?'

Hec Jones turned and headed towards the rear door. 'Now!'

Both men walked out into the night.

18

By the time Matt Fallen and his deputy Elmer Hook had followed the wagon-wheel tracks to the back of the Golden Garter the wagon and its two venomous occupants had long gone. The marshal wiped the sweat from his features and rested a hand on the gates of the saloon's fenced yard. A lantern on the back wall provided the light and the information that both law officers required.

'Two of 'em, Marshal,' Elmer said as he carefully moved across the yard and looked down at the bootprints in the soft sand. They led from the rear door to where the wagon had stood. 'Just like ya figured.'

'A pair of well-worn boots and a pair of town shoes,' Fallen observed. He sighed. 'We've got ourselves two very different partners in crime, Elmer.'

'Ya reckon that this killer's partner works in the Golden Garter, Marshal?'

'Works in there, or maybe owns it.'

'That covers a lotta folks,' Elmer said. 'There gotta be three or four bartenders working in there. Who owns the Golden Garter?'

'Nate Bean, I think.'

'I always suspected it was him behind all this.'

Fallen placed his own boot against the shoe-print in the sand. Fallen's foot was at least two inches longer.

'That ain't Nate's shoe-mark,' he said. 'Not unless Nate has started to fold his feet up inside his shoes. His feet are as big as mine.'

'Then it's one of the barkeeps,' Elmer opined with a nod.

Fallen exhaled and coughed in a bid to rid his lungs of the smoke he had choked on back at the fire-stricken livery stable. He looked back at the glowing sky behind them, then at his deputy once again.

'Which one though?'

'We ain't gonna find that out until we catches him.'

The marshal turned and looked at the maze of fences and buildings in the opposite direction. So many red-brick and wooden structures that went on as far as the eye could see.

'And they went thataway, Elmer,' Fallen pointed.

Elmer's jaw dropped as he stood next to his superior. 'Where'd ya reckon they're headed? Ain't a lot of things on that side of town 'ceptin' a few fancy houses and the courthouse.'

Fallen rubbed his neck thoughtfully. 'By the looks of the tracks the wagon didn't pick nothing up from here. The grooves ain't no deeper after it left here than they were when it arrived.'

Elmer scratched his head. 'Could these two varmints be going to get something from over yonder? Something they needs a wagon to carry?'

Fallen nodded. 'Yep. They must be going to get something. Why else would they steal Clem's wagon? If they were only hightailing it out of town they would have just taken horses. Horses are a damn sight faster and easier to handle than a two-horse wagon. Yep. They have to be going to get something heavy and valuable, OK.'

'I'm fair tuckered out, Marshal,' Elmer admitted. 'We needs us a pair of horses to keep track with them critters or we'll never catch up with 'em.'

'You're dead right,' Fallen said. 'Cut down the alley to Front Street. A couple of Luke Sutton's horses are still hitched up down there. Get two of them and bring them back here.'

Elmer was about to do as he had been ordered when he paused and looked at the marshal. A wry smile cut across his features.

'Ya must be as tired as I am, Marshal,' he remarked.

Fallen glanced at the flashing teeth. 'Why would you figure that, Elmer?'

Elmer waved a finger at Fallen. 'I recall ya telling me a long time back that the only reason ya become a lawman was so that ya didn't have to ride horses too much.'

Fallen pushed the deputy in the direction of the alley. 'Go get them horses, Elmer.' He grinned. 'I'll force myself to ride one of them.'

Elmer saluted. 'Ya better hold on good and tight.'

As the deputy disappeared into the dark, unlit alley which led to Front Street, Fallen's expression changed. Suddenly he was aware that he and his smiling sidekick were getting close to the man or men they sought. Men who would not yield easily. The marshal pulled his gun from its holster and checked that it was fully loaded.

'This is going to be real rough going,' he muttered to himself as his eyes continued to stare at the glowing sky far behind them. 'If I'm not careful this could turn into a bloodbath.'

★　★　★

Even in the moonlight it looked no less impressive. Sol Hancock's home was

163

sturdy, unlike so many other buildings within the boundaries of War Smoke. It was mostly red brick with two-inch-thick oak doors to front and rear. A mansion by any standards but for all its strength it had a weakness that the wagon driver knew only too well.

Hec Jones eased back on the reins and stopped the pair of horses outside the rear of the big house. He looped the reins around the brake pole, rubbed his hands together and gave a chuckle. Texas Tom McCree had sat silently beside him for the twenty-minute journey through the town's twisting back streets. Slowly the outlaw rose from the driving board, swung one of his legs over the side of the high wagon and clambered down to the ground.

Jones jumped down beside him. 'What ya think?'

For a few moments the outlaw said nothing as his cruel eyes absorbed the impressive proportions of the edifice before them. He ran a gloved thumb along his unshaven jawbone and shook his head.

'We'll never bust in there without waking half of War Smoke, Jones,' McCree said. 'It's built like a fortress.'

'I told ya I got keys,' Jones snapped. 'No wonder ya got so much bounty on ya head. Ya just plain dumb.'

'Still don't figure on what ya bin telling me as on the level, runt,' the outlaw grunted. 'Don't look like there's no fortune to be had in there. Just a lot of fancy chairs like ya can find in most whorehouses.'

'That's what everyone thinks when they set eyes on this place, Texas Tom.' Jones started to walk towards the building with the outlaw on his heels. 'But they don't know the secret that I know.'

McCree grunted. He was not impressed or even convinced by words he had accepted until now without question from the man who had brought him here.

With narrowed eyes McCree watched as Jones ignored the solid door and moved to a large bush growing against the wall. He pushed the bush aside to reveal another, far smaller door. It was cut low and wide.

Jones looked over his shoulder at McCree. 'Now are ya starting to wise up, Texas Tom?'

McCree did not reply. He moved to the barkeep's shoulder and watched as Jones selected one of the keys.

'That looks like a key for the rear door!' the outlaw exclaimed.

Jones smiled wide. 'It is, Texas. But it also fits this door here.'

McCree watched as Jones pushed the key into the lock and turned it. The door opened inwards. Jones nodded.

'That's the key ya took from the widow woman.'

The outlaw bent down and trailed Hec Jones into the darkness of the hidden corridor. He struck a match and found a lamp close to the entrance. McCree touched the wick, turned the brass wheel and lowered the stained-glass funnel.

The almost golden light revealed

another door. This one was far more solid than the first. It was, like the main doors of the house, constructed of solid oak. Reinforced bolts added to the security of the hand-carved door.

McCree rested a hand on the door and stared at it. 'I'm starting to have new faith in ya, Jones.'

'The best is yet to come,' Jones said. He checked the two remaining keys in his hands and chose the larger. He then pushed it into the brass lock and turned it slowly. The muffled sound of a tumbler being released came to the ears of the two men standing in the corridor.

'I'm startin' to think that it was worth killing all them folks,' McCree drawled in his sharp Texan accent. 'I'm startin' to believe there is a hidden fortune in here.'

Jones hesitated for a moment. 'What would ya do if I was lying to ya, Texas Tom?'

'Kill ya!' came the swift reply.

'It's a good job I'm tellin' ya the truth then.'

'Damn right!' the outlaw said firmly. 'One more killin' wouldn't make me lose any sleep.'

The man who had spent the previous few years as a bartender in the Golden Garter felt a bead of sweat trace down his face from his hatband. His heart quickened as he started to think the unthinkable.

What if Sol Hancock had moved his hidden stash of loot?

'Help me pull this 'un back, Texas Tom! It's mighty heavy!'

Both men hauled the door towards them. It felt as though it weighed far more than either of them would have thought possible. Rusted hinges fought them every inch of the way.

'This ain't bin opened for quite a while, Jones,' the outlaw observed. 'That's gotta be a good sign. Right?'

'Right!' Jones agreed.

At last they had it open wide enough for them to pass through into another corridor. McCree held the lamp and Jones led the way around a brick corner. Light danced on the walls which surrounded them. Then they were faced with another solid brick wall and yet another door.

This one was the most impressive of the three. It was of solid steel and had obviously been made long before the house was built above it. Few banks could have boasted anything quite so elaborate.

It was almost circular with a wheel and a small keyhole in its middle.

'Where in tarnation did the mayor get this damn thing?' the outlaw asked curiously. 'I ain't never seen anything like this outside a real bank.'

'That's exactly where Sol Hancock got it. A bank,' Jones answered. 'He owned shares in a bank over in California for a few years until there was a run on it and the damn thing went bust. Leastways, that was Sol's story. I reckon he just stole the money and come running over the border.'

McCree ran his free hand over the steel door. It was like a mirror in the lamplight.

'Ya mean he had this thing brought here?'

'Yep!' Jones pushed the key into the lock. 'Had it hauled to War Smoke over the mountains and placed down here before he had the rest of the house built above it.'

The outlaw sighed. 'That man was sure tricky.'

Jones turned the key clockwise. He then spun the wheel to his left until it stopped. Then he turned the key back.

'That's it!' he declared and pulled the door away from its steel frame. It was so well-balanced neither man heard a sound as it opened wide.

Texas Tom McCree's eyes widened as he pushed the lamp into the vault. 'Would ya look at all that money! I never seen so much money in all my days!'

Hec Jones sighed in relief. Hancock's fortune was still where he had last seen it.

Boxes of gold and silver coins were stacked inside the dark chamber next to piles of cash close to the door. McCree grabbed handfuls of the green bills and stuffed his pockets until they were full.

'There has to be a fortune in here, runt,' the outlaw drooled. 'A real honest to goodness fortune.'

'Honesty had nothing to do with it, Texas,' Jones corrected as he clambered into the cavernous vault. 'Reckon we just found ourselves the end of the rainbow.'

'How much do ya reckon this is worth, Jones?' McCree placed the lamp inside the shining interior of the vault. He then dragged the nearest box, filled with golden coins, to the lip of the vault.

'Thousands!' Jones guessed.

McCree strained but managed to lift the box. 'I'll take this back up to the wagon.'

Jones pulled another of the boxes out of the vault. It was filled with silver coins. He then hauled another out filled with golden half-eagles. Then another.

'There's even more here now than when I worked for Hancock,' Jones whispered to himself. 'Enough to make two men stinkin' rich.'

'Hey, runt!' McCree's voice echoed within the tunnel.

Jones glanced back.

McCree squeezed the trigger of his Colt. A dazzling flash blinded the bartender as the bullet spewed from the outlaw's gun barrel. The sound was deafening in the narrow confines of the basement but Hec Jones did not hear it.

The bullet had gone straight through Jones's heart long before the sound reached him.

The outlaw blew down the barrel of his smoking weapon and walked toward the lamplight and the body sprawled out across the mouth of the vault floor.

'Sorry, Jones! Ya really should know that ya just can't trust nobody these days!'

19

The two riders had trailed the wagon-wheel grooves halfway across War Smoke through every twisting lane and alley. The marshal turned to his fellow lawman and pointed at the tailgate of the wagon protruding from the back of the large red-brick house.

'There it is!'

'I see it, Marshal,' Elmer responded. 'Say! Ain't that Sol's place?'

'Yep,' Fallen confirmed.

'What ya figure them no-good head-stompin' dirty lowdown killers want there?'

'Whatever it is I'll bet it's worth a tidy sum, Elmer.'

Both riders eased back on their reins and brought their horses to a standstill. They were still twenty yards from the building. Fallen dismounted and tossed his reins to Elmer.

'You head on round to the other side of the house!' he ordered. 'When the shooting starts, come running!'

'I'll come running and shootin', Marshal!' Elmer nodded as he wrapped the marshal's reins around his saddle horn. 'Ya know ya can count on me.'

Fallen bit his lip. 'Just come running, boy! I've seen your shooting skills and I don't want to get plugged by my own deputy.'

Elmer looked offended. 'I'll shoot up into the air.'

Fallen nodded, slapped the tail of Elmer's mount and then ran into the shadows cast by the mansion once owned by Sol Hancock. Trees and bushes came to within twenty yards of the rear of the handsome house. Fallen moved silently between them, keeping away from the bright moonlight which he knew could betray him.

He knelt beside a stout tree, drew his Colt and cocked its hammer. From his vantage point he could now see the whole of the wagon clearly. The tailgate was indeed down. There were three boxes on the flatbed. Fallen gritted his teeth and tried to work out what was in the boxes. Whatever it was it had to be worth killing a lot of people for.

Fallen was about to raise himself up and move closer when he saw a tall unfamiliar figure emerge from the rear of the house. The marshal rose to his full height, steadied himself and moved further into the shadows. The moonlight illuminated the face of Tom McCree but Fallen had never seen this man before.

He wondered who he could be looking at.

His eyes screwed up. He focused on the heavy box in the arms of the stranger. The man was staggering under the sheer weight of the box.

With his gun levelled at the stranger, Fallen raced from the shadows into the bright moonlight.

'I'd stay right there if I was you,' the marshal recommended.

Texas Tom McCree stopped and

stood motionless with the box in his hands. His eyes burned across the distance between them until they fixed on Fallen's tin star.

'Ya talking to me, Marshal?' McCree growled.

Fallen moved closer.

'Damn right I am!'

McCree laughed and dropped the box. The sound of coins filled the air.

'Ya a mighty big talker with that hogleg in ya hands, Marshal,' the outlaw spat. 'That how they do it in these parts?'

Fallen stepped closer. He kept his gun trained on the stranger.

'Who the hell are you, mister?'

McCree took a deep breath, his chest swelled.

'They call me Texas Tom McCree,' he said proudly. 'Ya ever heard of me?'

Suddenly Matt Fallen's mind raced back to the wanted poster he had plucked from the dead bounty hunter who had gunned down Moose Coltrane. He recalled the words which had been printed beneath the price on the outlaw's head.

'Wanted for killing men, women and children!' Fallen repeated the words aloud. 'Dead or Alive!'

The smile faded from McCree's face. 'Ya got a good memory for details, Marshal. But it ain't gonna do ya no good at all 'coz I'm gonna kill ya like all the rest.'

'Mighty big talk, Texas Tom!' Fallen watched as the outlaw's gun hand began to close on the grip of the holstered Colt. The fingers were moving in a well-rehearsed manner which only expert gunslingers truly mastered.

'Ya must be real scared of old Texas Tom, Marshal,' McCree said bluntly. 'Only a yella coward would keep a gun aimed at someone like me. What's the matter? Scared of facing me in a showdown? Ya know that ya ain't got a chance of beating me in a fair fight. I reckon I could outdraw and kill ya even now before ya pulls that trigger.'

'Maybe so,' Fallen allowed.

McCree laughed and looked over his shoulder and then back at the man with the tin star. 'I even bet ya got another gun aimed at my back.'

Fallen ignored the outlaw's words.

'Where's your partner?' asked Fallen. His eyes searched the area for the other man who, he knew, had come to this place with the outlaw.

'Dead!' McCree chuckled.

'You kill him the same way that you killed all them other innocent folks, Texas Tom?' Fallen queried. 'You stove his head in as well?'

'Nope. I just put a bullet through his heart.' McCree tilted his head and smiled. 'The head-crushin' was Jones's idea of killin', Marshal. He reckoned it would keep ya chasing ya tail long enough for us to bust in to the mayor's hidden vault and make our getaway. Jones was wrong.'

'Jones?' Fallen repeated the name. 'Hec Jones?'

'Damn it all!' The outlaw shrugged. 'Ya really are darn good at ya job.'

Fallen caught a glimpse of Elmer beyond the threatening figure of McCree. The deputy was holding his rifle with its barrel aimed at the stars above them.

'Get moving!' the marshal ordered. 'I'm taking you in.'

Defiantly McCree remained where he was. 'I ain't gonna be jailed just so ya can hang me, Marshal. Ya want me then ya gotta shoot me but I don't reckon that's ya way.'

Fallen knew the man was right. He could not kill even the most loathsome of creatures in cold blood. There was an unwritten code of honour that lawmen like Fallen lived by. If McCree would not budge there was only one thing he could do. Ignoring all the risks involved, Fallen would have to do this the hard way. The most dangerous of ways.

'Showdown?' The marshal muttered the word.

'Yep!' McCree nodded. 'I just hope ya boy back there don't backshoot me after I've killed ya, Marshal.'

'I thought that you would be fast

enough to kill him as well, Texas Tom,' riposted Fallen with a smirk.

The outlaw flexed his fingers above his gun grip and smiled at his opponent. It was not the smile of a man with humour in his heart. It was the sickening smile of one who would kill just to satisfy his diabolical soul.

The lawman took a deep breath and dropped his weapon into its holster. For a few seconds both men stared at one another in the eerie moonlight. Then Fallen shouted.

'Draw!'

Without a second's hesitation, McCree went for his Colt.

Both men's guns cleared their well-oiled holsters at exactly the same time. Both free hands fanned the hammers within a mere split second of each other.

White lightning spewed out in both directions.

It was loud enough to awaken the dead. The ear-splitting sound of bullets blasting from barrels rocked the area behind the mayor's house. The acrid stench of gunsmoke filled the air. But only Matt Fallen was able to fan his gun hammer a second time.

The fine accuracy of Fallen's first shot had lifted Texas Tom McCree off his feet. The second shot pushed the outlaw's already dead body even further away. Like a large rag doll McCree flew backwards through the air and landed in a crumpled heap in front of the deputy, who had come running.

Elmer stopped abruptly and looked at the dead man. The eyes of the outlaw were wide open, staring at things only the dead can see. Elmer gulped and licked his dry lips as the marshal walked towards him with the smoking .45 in his hand.

'Reckon the reward money will come in useful, Elmer,' Fallen said coldly. 'We could buy ourselves a new coffee pot and some fresh beans to put in it.'

'Why'd ya take such a risk, Marshal?' Elmer asked. 'Ya should have just plugged him. He might have bin faster than he looked.'

'I figured his hands might be a tad sore after carrying them heavy boxes of coins, Elmer.' Fallen sighed. 'Nothing worse than sore hands when you're trying to draw your gun fast.'

The shaking deputy leaned over and looked hard at the face of Texas Tom. He wiped the sweat from his own face with his left hand and ran it down the outside of his britches.

'Glory be! Ya shot him clean between the eyes two whole times, Marshal. I never seen such shooting.'

'Between the eyes?' Fallen dropped his gun into his holster and looked down at the outlaw's twisted body. He gave it a kick and then shrugged. 'I ought to get my gun balanced, I was aiming for his heart, Elmer.'

'No wonder ya missed it.' The deputy smiled. 'Trash like this 'un ain't got no hearts to hit, Marshal.'

Finale

The morning had started hot and was getting hotter with every passing heartbeat. People began to fill the streets of War Smoke with a confidence they had been lacking for weeks. News that the marshal had managed to dispatch the maniac killer had spread faster than wildfire. There was a look of relief in the faces of those who paced the town's boardwalks as Matt Fallen and Elmer neared Doc's office en route for their own.

The door opened and the tired old medical practitioner walked out. He sat down on the chair beside his window beneath the porch overhang. The marshal and deputy paused and smiled.

'Mornin', Doc,' Elmer said politely.

'Elmer.' Doc nodded.

'You look tired, Doc,' Fallen remarked.

'I ought to be.' Doc pulled his pipe

from his pocket, placed it between his teeth and sighed. His fingers fumbled in his vest pocket, located a match and struck it along the side of the chair. He sucked the flame into the pipe bowl and allowed the smoke to drift from his lips. 'I spent all night tending them wounded Lazy D boys.'

Elmer tapped the marshal's arm. 'Why don't ya stand a spell and talk with old Doc? I'll go put a fresh pot of coffee on the stove, Marshal. Nothing like a good cup of coffee to start the day with.'

Fallen and Doc watched the deputy make his way down to the office before they spoke.

'A good cup of coffee,' Fallen smiled.

'I don't see how you've lived so long, Matt.' Doc smiled as he puffed. 'Elmer's one of the nicest folks there is, but when it comes to coffee . . . '

'Yeah, Elmer's coffee is a little strong most days, Doc.'

Doc pulled the pipe from his mouth and pointed its stem at the long-legged

Hudson Parker as the gunfighter crossed the wide sandy street on his way towards the bank.

'Who is that, Matt? I saw him wandering around Front Street a few times yesterday.'

Fallen turned his head, looked at Hudson Parker and shrugged. He returned his gaze to the seated doctor.

'I don't know, Doc. He looks like another of those bounty hunters or drifters we've bin plagued with lately!'

'He's headed for the bank.' Doc raised a bushy eyebrow. 'Ya don't think he might be a bank-robber, do ya?'

Fallen sat down on the sill of the window. 'If we hear shooting comin' from the bank, I'll go take a look.'

Hired gunfighter Hudson Parker had timed his walk from the hotel well. As he stepped up on the boardwalk outside the bank, rancher Bruno Jackson was walking out into the sunshine with a bag of coins in his left hand.

Both men stopped and looked at one another. Parker nodded and then led

Jackson into the Red Dog. They moved without utterance into the bar and sat in the same seats as they had occupied the previous day.

The bartender looked at them across the empty room. 'Ya want whiskey, boys?'

'Not for me, barkeep,' Hudson replied. 'Mr Jackson will partake though.'

Jackson opened the bag under the table. He carefully counted out the golden coins required for the first instalment of the payment he and Parker had agreed.

Hudson accepted the $500 in gold coin and slid it into his deep trail-coat pockets. He moved away from the chair and table as the bartender arrived with the whiskey.

'I'll have me a bottle of ya best when I gets back,' Parker told the bartender.

Jackson watched as Pete, his white apron wrapped around his middle, returned to the long counter. He downed the drink in one swallow.

'Nervous, Mr Jackson?'

'Don't underestimate Matt Fallen, Parker,' the rancher said fearfully. 'Boot Hill is filled with a whole bunch of dumb bastards who did.'

The hired gun checked his pair of matched pistols and gave a spooky smile down at the seated rancher. He slid the pistols into their beautifully hand-tooled holsters and pushed the tails of his long coat over their gleaming grips.

'Matt Fallen never met anyone as fast as me, *amigo*.'

Jackson snapped his fingers at the bartender for him to bring more whiskey to his table. He then looked up into the hard, cruel features of the man who, he knew, meant every word he uttered.

'Just heed my words, Parker,' he urged.

'Just count out the other five hundred bucks.' Hudson Parker smiled again, touched the brim of his hat and strolled off towards the saloon doorway.

'It's as good as done.'

Front Street was busier than it had been for weeks. It was as though all the folks who had feared the unknown slayer suddenly realized that they were in need not only of provisions but of sun on their skin. There were so many people that the tall, gaunt figure with the matched guns on his hips went almost unnoticed as he made his way slowly along the middle of the street in the direction of the marshal's office.

Buckboards wove their way around the riders who guided their mounts in all directions. It was as though everyone within fifty miles had suddenly descended upon War Smoke at the very same moment. The town had not been as busy for months. Men, women and children crossed paths without a care in their hearts.

Yet if any of them had taken the time to look at the grim gunfighter and the deadly expression carved into his features they would have known that trouble had not quite gone from the remote Nevada town.

Marshal Fallen stood up and stretched his tired arms. He touched his hat-brim to the doctor and began to walk the short distance to his office and the noxious beverage his deputy was creating.

'Fallen!' a voice called out from amid the crowd that filled the street.

The marshal paused, turned on his heel and looked in the direction from where the unfamiliar voice had come. He rested a hand on the nearest wooden upright and screwed up his eyes. The crowd was dense. A sea of human bodies moved before his eyes like waves.

'Fallen!' the voice called out again. 'Git ready to die, Fallen!'

People of every shape and size began to rush away from the man who stood defiantly in the middle of Front Street with his hands above his guns. It did not take long for the street to clear completely. Every store and saloon had filled with the overflow of people who instinctively knew what was about to occur.

Matt Fallen sighed. He stared at the man who had called his name. It was the same tall man whom Doc had pointed out to him only five minutes earlier.

'You say that you're going to kill me, stranger?' The marshal stepped down from the boardwalk and walked to the middle of the wide thoroughfare. Each step was designed to calculate the distance between them. He slowly lowered his right hand so that his thumb could flick the safety loop off his gun hammer.

His fingers rested upon his hip.

To his dismay, there was no safety loop.

No gun hammer.

No gun or belt.

Fallen suddenly realized that he had not put his gunbelt on after venturing out an hour earlier to the café for breakfast. It had seemed pointless to the man who had already out-gunned Texas Tom McCree.

Sweat ran down the side of the

marshal's face. It trickled over his cheek and across his jawbone.

'What you want, stranger?' Fallen asked.

'What do I want, Marshal?' Parker smiled. 'I just want to kill ya! Nothing else!'

Fallen rested his hands on his hips. 'Killing an unarmed man is a hanging offence in these parts.'

Hudson Parker laughed. 'With you dead, I don't figure they'll try to hang me. Didn't ya see the way they all hightailed it off the street? Nope! Nobody will hang me, Mr Fallen!'

Fallen raised his hands.

'But I'm not packing a gun.'

'Damned if I care!' Parker's hands were fast. So fast that they managed to draw both guns from their holsters before the marshal could utter another word. Fallen knew that he had only one chance of survival and that was to make the gunfighter's target as small as possible. That was not easy for a man built like Matt Fallen. He turned sideways on but still felt the lead hit him off his feet.

He crashed into the sand. It was as if a branding-iron had been thrust into him. Helplessly, Fallen looked across at Parker as the man started to walk towards him. The hired gunman cocked the hammers of both his guns again and grinned.

'Don't fret none, Marshal! I'll finish this clean!'

Then the sound of another gun being fired filled the almost empty street. Fallen's eyes darted to his left and he saw Elmer standing outside his office with a smoking gun in his hand. The marshal looked back at Parker.

Hudson Parker continued walking for two more strides of his long legs. He then paused. His guns fell from his hands and he stared down at his shirt front. Blood covered its fabric as he dropped on to his knees.

Then he fell on to his face.

'Are ya OK, Marshal?' Elmer called out as he ran to the wounded lawman.

Before Fallen could answer he saw Doc rush to him as well with his battered old bag in his hands.

'Don't move for a while, Matt!' Doc ordered as he knelt beside him. 'Let me check ya out!'

Fallen looked at his deputy with the gun in his hands. 'You hit him, Elmer! Dead centre, boy!'

Elmer looked at the gun. 'This is your gun, Marshal. I reckon ya right about it needing balancing. I was aiming at his head.'

Fallen shook his head. 'Least you hit him. You saved my life, Elmer.'

'Ya lucky, Matt,' Doc said, as he and the deputy helped the marshal back to his feet. 'The bullet went clean through ya side. We'll get ya to my office and I'll clean ya up.'

With Fallen's arms around Doc's shoulders on one side and Elmer on the other, the three men moved as one across the sand toward Doc's office.

As they reached the boardwalk, the deputy cleared his throat.

'Seein' that I kinda saved ya life, can I borrow me a dollar, Marshal? I got me a date with Miss Peggy from the Red Dog.'

'She the one with the teeth, Elmer?'

'That's the one, Doc.' The deputy began to blush. 'The real pretty one.'

'White teeth,' Fallen added.

'Store-bought teeth,' Doc chuckled.

'No, they ain't store-bought. They is real teeth, Doc!'

Fallen paused with the two men to either side of him. His eyes narrowed as he watched Bruno Jackson mount his horse outside the saloon and spur.

'What ya lookin' at, Marshal?'

Matt Fallen eased his deputy from under his armpit. He looked at Elmer and then to the body of Parker lying in a pool of blood-soaked sand.

'Go check the pockets of that gunfighter, Elmer! I got me a feeling he was paid to kill me,' Fallen said. 'You can keep anything you find after we pay Doc and the undertaker.'

Elmer ran to the body.

'Ya think that long-legged gunslinger was paid, Matt?' Doc asked. 'By whom?'

Fallen looked to the fleeing Jackson and then back at the small man who was holding him up.

'It'll keep, Doc. It'll keep.'

We do hope that you have enjoyed reading this large print book.

Did you know that all of our titles are available for purchase?

We publish a wide range of high quality large print books including:
Romances, Mysteries, Classics
General Fiction
Non Fiction and Westerns

Special interest titles available in large print are:
The Little Oxford Dictionary
Music Book, Song Book
Hymn Book, Service Book

Also available from us courtesy of Oxford University Press:
Young Readers' Dictionary
(large print edition)
Young Readers' Thesaurus
(large print edition)

For further information or a free brochure, please contact us at:
Ulverscroft Large Print Books Ltd.,
The Green, Bradgate Road, Anstey,
Leicester, LE7 7FU, England.
Tel: (00 44) **0116 236 4325**
Fax: (00 44) **0116 234 0205**

PATHS OF DEATH

P. McCormac

He had done with killing. That was all in the past. Zacchaeus Wolfe was a peaceful dirt farmer. But the Lazy K didn't like sodbusters. The Kerfoots owned the range . . . and the law. His little farm did not fit into their plans. So old man Barrett Kerfoot and his five sons, backed by a full complement of cowboys, began to push Zacchaeus. But they'd find out the hard way what it was to have a curly wolf by the tail . . .

THE GUNS OF CALEB JONES

Alan C. Porter

Caleb Jones rode into Desert Bluffs to make peace with his daughter whom he had not seen in twenty years. But Aguilar's raiders, from across the Mexican border, denied him the opportunity, killing her and taking his granddaughters. Then as Caleb rode in to get them back, guns blazing, it seemed that this explosive rescue mission into Mexico was doomed from the start. But Caleb wouldn't accept defeat lying down. When his guns spoke, men listened or died . . .

BRAND 8: DEVIL'S GOLD

Neil Hunter

Jason Brand's new assignment has him pitched against Kwo Han, Chinese Tong Master, in a struggle to gain control of Confederate gold, lost for over twenty years. Brand has to battle the odds, violence and betrayal as he moves from New Mexico to Yucatan, gaining a new partner and facing blazing action. In his return to duty Brand brings his own justice to the lawbreakers — and they are no match for his deadly skills!